The Christmas Concierge

The Christmas
Concierge

BETH KENDRICK

TULE
PUBLISHING

Dedication

For Jackie Fulcher, who sits where she wants

Chapter One

HOLIDAY SMITH CLOSED her eyes and inhaled the scents of the season—chocolate and cinnamon tinged with an undertone of desperation. Shoppers were packed five deep at the counter of the patisserie, everyone flushed and shifting their shopping bags from arm to arm as they tried to catch the attention of the counter staff. Holiday felt a bead of sweat trickling down under her jacket and scarf, but adrenaline surged as she caught a server's eye: *Victory is nigh.*

"Hi, I'll take the Bûche de Noël cake, please." She had to yell over the din of the crowd.

The server shook his head and turned up both hands in a shrug. "We just ran out."

Her surge of adrenaline soured into panic. "What? But I need it. Please, it's urgent."

"Come back tomorrow morning," the server advised. "We usually run out of them by noon this time of year."

Holiday fumbled in her handbag for her wallet. "I'll pay double. Triple! Name your price."

"Lady, I told you, we're out. But if you're that freaked out—"

"I am."

"Try asking that guy over there." The server pointed out

a tall man in a black overcoat heading toward the exit. "He bought the last one."

Holiday nodded her thanks over her shoulder as she dodged and weaved through the throngs of crazed Christmas shoppers. "Excuse me. *Excuse me!*"

The man didn't hear her. Or at least, he pretended not to.

"Hey! You with the Bûche de Noël! Freeze!"

He did, with his hand on the brass push bar and one foot poised to hit the slushy doormat.

"Thank you, sir. I need a quick word with you." The outdoor air blasted in, chilly and damp against her overheated cheeks.

The man turned around and Holiday took his measure in a nanosecond—good-looking, late thirties, expensive haircut, purposeful stride. Kind eyes.

"Do I know you?" he asked.

"No." She summoned her sweetest smile. "But you sure would be doing me a favor if you'd let me buy that cake from you."

He clutched the white cardboard pastry box a bit closer to his chest. "I'm bringing this to a dinner party tonight."

She nodded. "You know what else is great for dinner parties? Tiramisu."

"But this is a special cake, as you're obviously aware."

"Oh, I'm aware. The finest French chocolate, fresh berries, and edible gold leaf on the 'bark.'" She swiped through her phone until her banking app came up. "I'll give you double what you paid for it. You can come back tomorrow before noon and get a fresh one."

He glanced out at the pedestrians bustling by on Amsterdam Avenue, clearly in a hurry to join them. "Why can't *you* come back tomorrow?"

"Because I need to present this cake to an editor-in-chief downtown in two hours." Holiday pointed to the box in his hands. "I'm going to ask for a huge favor and I need to ply her with baked goods."

He paused. "What's the favor?"

"Is that really relevant?"

"It is if you're trying to coerce me out of a cake I already bought and paid for."

She motioned him to come closer and lowered her voice conspiratorially. "I'm going to ask the editor to get me a signed copy of a novel written by an author who hasn't made any public appearances in ten years. Total recluse. This editor bought his first book fifteen years ago, and she's the only person who can get in touch with him. I read an interview with her in *Publishers Marketplace*, and she mentioned that the Bûche de Noël from this bakery is her favorite dessert on Earth. And very hard to get."

"Who's the author?"

She glimpsed the curiosity in his eyes, and she knew she had him. "I'll tell you if you hand over the cake. What do you say?"

He wavered, his fingers tightening around the pastry box.

"Listen. I can tell you're very busy and important, and frankly, so am I. Neither of us has time for chitchat and, also, we're screwing up the line." She averted her gaze from the customers glowering at them. "Let's make a deal and be on our way."

One corner of his mouth tugged up in a smile. "All right, you're on."

Holiday opened her Venmo account and braced herself for the hit her petty cash fund was about to take.

"But you can keep your money," he said. "I give you the cake, you give me your phone number."

Her head snapped up. "Seriously?"

"You wanted to negotiate. I'm negotiating." His smile amped up into a grin. "Let's meet again when we do have time for chitchat."

Holiday brushed back her hair and fluttered her eyelashes just a bit. "If you insist."

"I insist. Say, dinner tomorrow night? You can tell me how it went with the bakery bribes at the publishing house."

She stifled a sigh and stopped fluttering—both inside and out. "I wish I could, but I'm booked tomorrow night."

Her refusal only spurred his determination. "How about Friday, then?" he countered. "Or Saturday? I have three holiday parties coming up this weekend—I'll tell you all about them and you can take your pick."

The sweet smells of the bakery gave way to a note of bitterness as she extracted a business card from her pocket. "That sounds amazing, and I'd love to go . . . but I'm booked solid for the next week."

He glanced down at her name, number, and job title. "'Christmas Concierge'?"

"That's right." She eased the bakery box out of his grasp.

"I track down hard-to-find gifts for the most discerning clients all over the world."

He gave her his full attention. "Like who?"

"That's confidential."

"So you can find anything?" he pressed.

"Anything. Wishes granted from the heart, presented with panache, and delivered on time. Guaranteed."

He glanced down at his suit and tie, clearly realizing that he had lived his life all wrong. "That's a real job?"

"So says my accountant."

"And your real name is Holiday?"

She nodded. "It was clearly meant to be. And again, I am so sorry because I'd love to stay and talk, but I have an editor to bribe." She ducked past him and out to the hustle and bustle of Manhattan's Upper West Side.

"What about dinner?" He fell into step beside her.

She paused and turned to face him so she could scrutinize his expression. "We'll have to take a rain check until January second."

And there it was—the flicker of dismissal and disinterest. Even though it was already the end of December, so much was packed in between now and New Year's that January second might as well be six months away. The moment he realized she couldn't accompany him to his many parties, his interest pivoted from the personal to the professional.

"You know, I've been looking for something special for my parents," he ventured. "Do you think—"

"Sorry, I'm booked solid for the rest of this season. Email me and we can get you on the waitlist for next Christmas."

She nodded in sympathy at his evident dismay. "What can I say? I'm a woman in demand."

He shook his head. "This is not how I saw this conversation going."

"You and me both." She straightened up and resumed walking toward the subway station. "But thanks for the cake."

"I'll be following up on that rain check on January second," he called after her.

"You have my number." She clutched the pastry box close and dashed for the stairs leading down to the subway. "Happy holidays!"

He yelled something in reply, but his voice was lost amid the chatter of the crowd and the clatter of the express train barreling down the tracks.

Chapter Two

"YOU GOT IT." Nora ran her hand over the cover of the hardback novel. "You actually got it."

"Don't sound so surprised. Was there ever any doubt?" Holiday took the book back from her sister, rewrapped the acid-free tissue paper, and tucked it safely into her suitcase. Her apartment looked clean and minimalist to the point of being sparse—probably because it was more of a home base than a true home. She had bought the two-bedroom in a fancy northern Virginia high-rise as an investment and a place to crash between gift quests. Nora was forever bringing over throw pillows and scented candles in a futile attempt to cozy the place up, and Holiday didn't have the heart to discourage her. But the fact was, no matter how many fanciful Christmas gifts she procured, Holiday would always be a pragmatist with nary a scrap of cozy in her DNA. Hence, the northern Virginia address—close to her family, easy access to an international airport, and only occasional snow delays during the crucial months of November and December.

Nora sipped from her glass of pinot noir. "Was there ever any doubt that you could weasel your way all the way to a nonforged signature from Benny Bruneto? The guy who makes J. D. Salinger look like a cruise director? Uh, yeah. I had doubt."

Holiday threw her a saucy wink. "They call me the Wish Granter."

"*And* you met a hot guy?"

She waved that away. "Yeah, but I'm never going to hear from that guy again."

"I bet you'll hear from him." Nora curled up on the sofa and tucked her feet under her legs.

Holiday smiled. "Bless your delusional little heart."

"Why is that so delusional?" Nora demanded. "If he bequeathed you his *bûche*, he must be seriously smitten."

"How many times have I been down this road?" Holiday threw up her hands. "Men don't like being abandoned this time of year. They want a date for the cocktail parties and family dinners and office gatherings."

"Don't generalize," her sister scolded. "I'm sure there are guys out there who couldn't care less if their girlfriends are out of town for—"

"All of November and December?" Holiday finished.

Nora nodded.

"Well, I have yet to find one of those guys." Holiday helped herself to a sip of her sister's wine. "And it's a shame, because this guy really was cute. And polite. And funny." She paused. "Plus, given the quality of his suit, I'd be willing to bet that his office party is going to be *really* swanky, with free-flowing top-shelf champagne and gourmet hors d'oeuvres."

"I know how you love hors d'oeuvres," Nora said.

"I do love them." Holiday sat on the sofa next to her sister. "But no. He'll go to the swanky parties by himself and some other woman will scoop him up and the two of them will live happily ever after, curling up by the fireside and eating Bûche de Noël every Christmas Eve."

Nora swatted her with the pillow. "Or he'll call you on January second."

Holiday didn't even deign to respond to that. "The good news is, I don't have time to worry about phone calls that will never come. I'm on a plane first thing tomorrow morning."

"Back to New York?"

"Iowa," Holiday corrected. "Pray for no weather delays in Cedar Rapids."

"What's in Cedar Rapids?"

"A Dandie Dinmont terrier puppy. I've got to pick him up from the breeder and deliver him to his new home in Los Angeles."

"I've never heard of a Dandie Dinmont terrier." Nora started Googling on her phone.

"Neither had I. You know why? Because they're incredibly hard to find. There are literally more pandas in the world right now than Dandie Dinmont terriers."

"Then how . . .?" Nora clapped her hand to her heart as a photo of an adorable, fluffy puppy materialized.

"Three days on the internet, dozens of phone calls, and filling out a puppy application that was basically the equivalent of applying to Harvard." Holiday winced at the memory. "I told my client I would do it, so I did. The Wish

Granter never gives up."

"I guess not. Good lord." Nora circled back to the more important questions: "So when you met with the editor, did you get to have any of the Bûche de Noël?"

"Yeah. It was delicious, but not as delicious as Mom's cinnamon rolls are going to be."

Now it was Nora's turn to give a patronizing smile. "Bless your delusional little heart."

Holiday turned her face away. "What?"

"You and I both know—we *alllll* know—that you're not going to be home for Christmas."

"Yes, I am!" Holiday got to her feet and zipped up her suitcase with more vigor than necessary. "This year is different."

Nora took a beat and let Holiday's words sink in. "You say that every year."

"Yeah, but this time it's true. I cut back on my bookings this year."

"Mm-hmm." Nora put down her wineglass and folded her arms over her chest.

"I'm not lying! I am going to be there Christmas morning, shoving cinnamon rolls into my gob. I pinky promise." Holiday extended her little finger.

Nora refused to join pinkies. "Don't make promises you can't keep. Just be honest and say you'll roll in on the twenty-sixth or twenty-seventh, jet-lagged and sleep-deprived, as per usual." She held up her palm. "It's okay, we still love you. We'll keep the tree up."

"You're going to loot my stocking yet again, aren't you?"

Her sister grinned. "Consider it your late fee."

"You'll see," Holiday vowed. "I'm going to be in Mom and Dad's living room, looting *your* stocking before you're even awake on Christmas morning." Her cell phone chimed. She glanced at the name on caller ID and headed for the hallway. "Hang on, I have to take this."

When she reentered the bedroom a few minutes later, her sister read her expression immediately.

"You're missing Christmas again, aren't you?"

Holiday took a slow, deep breath. "No."

"Liar!"

"I just have to take a quick detour to Maine after Los Angeles."

"A little pitstop." Nora's eye roll was even more dramatic this time. "Maine and Virginia are practically next door."

"It's . . . I can't say no." Holiday put her hand on the wall to quell the sudden feeling of dizziness. "I owe this client whatever she asks for."

"And she's asking for Maine?"

"Someplace called Alemos Island, to be exact."

Nora was already online and researching. "Alemos Island? Oh, here we are, right off the coast. Current temperature is like absolute zero. You better pack a down parka and some furry earmuffs."

Fear seeped into Holiday's stomach. "Do you think it'll snow?"

"Yes," Nora stated decisively. "Maine plus December equals snow. It's basic math."

"Oh no." Holiday sank onto the sofa next to her sister.

"How much, do you think? Do you think there'll be a blizzard?"

"It's too soon to say." Nora patted the sofa cushion to indicate that Holiday should join her. "Don't worry, though. You'll be okay."

Holiday remained braced against the wall. "I've heard that before. I can't believe this is happening again."

"It's not," Nora declared.

"But what if—"

Nora held up a single, stern index finger. "It won't."

Holiday got to her feet, tamped down her nerves, and tried to match Nora's authoritative tone. "You're right, everything will be fine. I'll pack my parka. I'll rent an SUV with four-wheel drive. I'll check the weather religiously."

"Absolutely. Nothing can stand in the Wish Granter's way," Nora said. "This time."

"Amen, sister." Holiday strode to the front closet to retrieve her winter coat. "And Nora?"

"Yes?"

"In the immortal words of Bing Crosby, I *will* be home for Christmas."

Chapter Three

"STAND BY. I'M sending you some pictures of the target." At seventy-six years old, Mrs. Alice Penewate possessed the regal *hauteur* of old-world aristocracy along with the technological skills of an Apple engineer. Even over the phone, she commanded deference.

Holiday's eyebrows shot up as she studied the black-and-white photo downloading on the screen. "This is the guy?" She leaned forward over the hotel room's desk, upon which she'd assembled a packet of trail mix, a pen, and a legal pad to make notes about her last-minute mission. She closed her eyes for a moment and fought through a wave of jet lag before fortifying herself with a sip of coffee. Outside the fifth-floor window of the bland, corporate hotel room, the roar of airplane engines droned as late-night landings and takeoffs continued.

"Yes," Mrs. Penewate replied. "His name is Alex Sappier."

"But he's like fifteen years old."

"Don't be daft, darling. Those are his high school yearbook photos. My granddaughter Francie used to pore over those every day after school."

Holiday squinted at the grainy images of a fresh-faced

teenager with wavy black hair and a preppy polo shirt. "Do you have anything more recent?"

"Patience is a virtue," Mrs. Penewate admonished.

"Yes, ma'am." Holiday drummed her fingernails on the desktop as she waited for newer images to materialize.

Mrs. Penewate proceeded to bombard her with links to a series of news articles from Boston-area newspapers—"MIT Grad Makes Good in the Tech Sector," "A. Sappier Joins Board of Directors," and "Start-up Whiz Sells His Stake in Biotech Giant."

Holiday studied the photos of Alex Sappier, who was invariably decked out in a suit and tie. Although he was objectively handsome, he came across as remote. His expression was similar in every photo—tense and unsmiling to the point of looking grim.

"Your granddaughter was crushing on this guy?" Holiday dug the lone M&M out of the trail mix. "No offense, but he looks like the dude who'd call the cops to break up every party."

Mrs. Penewate inhaled sharply. "Are you questioning my granddaughter's judgment?"

"No, ma'am, I am not."

"Apparently, he was wretched working in the tech industry and so he pulled up stakes and moved to Maine."

Holiday started to ask why he would peace out to an island that was the climatic equivalent of a deep freezer, but then closed her mouth. Who cared why he moved to Maine? She didn't need to know his whole life story. She just needed to deliver him to his intended recipient and make it back to her parents' house for Christmas.

"Poor Francie has had a beastly year," Alice continued. "Her husband had an affair, the divorce was hellacious, and my sweet girl has just withered."

Holiday was dying to know how Mrs. Penewate was so sure that Francie would want to reunite with her high school crush, but again she managed to keep her mouth shut. Years of acting as a Christmas concierge had taught her that human desires were mysterious and often laden with a love and loss. She just needed to know the "who," "what," "where," and "when." The "why" was none of her business.

"A romantic pick-me-up is just what Francie needs for the new year," Alice continued. "She deserves to meet a man on her own level."

"You want it, you got it," Holiday assured her. "Let's go over the details. Where and when do you want all this to go down?"

"I've told Francie that I planned a surprise trip for her, but I haven't shared any of the details. She won't know she's going to Maine until I give her the boarding pass at the airport. I'm also going to give her an envelope with directions to the best hotel on the island." Mrs. Penewate paused. "That's where I'll be putting you up as well, of course."

"Thank you."

"Although from what I gather, there's only two or three lodging options, so 'the best' hotel may not be saying much."

Holiday glanced around at the beige carpet, beige wallpaper, and beige comforter in her current digs. "Don't you worry. I'm pretty low-maintenance."

"After you explain the situation to Mr. Sappier and ensure his cooperation, I'd like you to arrange a Christmas Eve meeting at the most romantic place possible."

"Um." Holiday stopped scribbling notes. "Christmas Eve?"

"That's correct."

Holiday slumped back in the desk chair, tilted her head upward, and closed her eyes.

"Is that a problem?" Mrs. Penewate's tone became crisper by the moment.

Holiday rubbed her forehead and forced herself to rejoin the conversation. "No, I can whip up an amazing dinner date, no problem, it's just . . . how long would you like me to stay and chaperone?"

"My heavens, they're adults. They don't need a chaperone, and I'm certain they won't want one."

Holiday opened her eyes to gaze at the beige ceiling as a tiny spark of hope rekindled. "So you wouldn't object if I left for the airport right after I introduce them?"

"Of course not." Alice seemed affronted by the very idea. "Go ahead and book an evening flight out of Boston that night."

"Thank you. I appreciate that."

"Then it's settled. I'll call Francie tomorrow and tell her to pack her bags. I'm so thrilled to be able to do this for her." There was another pause at the other end of the line. "And Holiday, I hate to bring this up, but . . ."

Holiday flinched in anticipation.

"This isn't going to be like last time, is it?" The old

dame's voice actually quavered. "I'm still a bit heartbroken, to be honest."

"No." Holiday squeezed her pen so hard her fingers ached. "I won't let you down again. I promise."

Chapter Four

B Y THE TIME Holiday made her way from Bangor International Airport to the rental car center, she'd zipped up her coat, pulled on fleece-lined gloves, and donned the fluffy earmuffs that Nora had insisted she take along. Her sister was right—as always. Holiday had thought she understood the concept of "cold," but Maine took it to a whole new level.

She had her driver's license ready as she approached the rental agent. "I have a reservation for Holiday Smith."

The employee typed in her information. "Ah yes, here you are." He printed out some documents for her to sign. "Your vehicle will be in parking spot 6B. It's a blue sedan."

Holiday froze. "I'm sorry . . . did you say 'sedan'?"

"That's correct. It's a four-door, midsize car." He listed the vehicle's make and model.

She shook her head so fast, her curls whipped against her cheeks. "There must be some mistake; I reserved an all-wheel-drive SUV."

The employee stopped making eye contact. "Um, yes, I see that. But I'm afraid that, due to the recent changes in the supply chain and transportation demands—"

"No, no, no." A shrill note of panic crept into her voice.

"I went out of my way to make sure that this didn't happen. I made promises, I have responsibilities, and I'm going to need all-wheel drive."

The employee rubbed his chin. "Where are you headed?"

"Alemos Island."

"Wow, you're really going off the beaten track, huh?"

"Yes." Her panic intensified. "And it's supposed to snow on and off over the next two days. I have a deep-rooted fear of blizzards."

The employee blinked. "Then why'd you come to Maine in the middle of winter?"

"It's a long story, and it ends with me needing all-wheel drive. So if you would kindly double-check your SUV availability . . ."

"Hang on. Let me ask the manager." The employee straightened his vest and picked up his phone.

"Thank you." Holiday tried to murmur calming mantras to herself while she waited. They didn't work.

The employee hung up, shaking his head. "Sorry."

"Please! There must be something we can do. I'll take anything." She smacked her palm against the countertop for emphasis. "Pickup truck, station wagon, whatever."

"I'd help you if I could. But we're completely out of stock." He gestured around the car rental building. "Everyone is, this time of year. You're lucky to get the sedan."

Holiday closed her eyes and spent a moment breathing deeply, which was even less effective than those stupid calming mantras. Then she opened her eyes and got back to business. "Does the sedan have snow tires, at least?"

His gaze shifted again. "Not exactly. But if you need to, you could always buy snow chains. Do you know how to put those on?"

She started to laugh at the sheer absurdity of the situation. "I do not, but I'm sure I can figure it out between divine intervention and YouTube." She took the key fob he offered, slung her carry-on over her shoulder, and set off in search of parking spot 6B.

BRIDGE FREEZES BEFORE ROAD

Holiday had seen similar road signs many times while traveling through the Northeast, but the message had never seemed quite so apt as it did now. The bridge stretching over the icy-gray Atlantic between the mainland and Alemos Island was, well, hopefully, not quite as old and rusty as it appeared.

The clear, sunny skies belied the frigid wind chill, and ice-crusted snowbanks rose up on either side of the two-lane highway, but Holiday felt grateful that at least the roads were currently dry. Warm air wafted out of the car's dashboard heat vents as her favorite travel podcast played over the speakers. All was calm, all was bright . . . for now.

The rural highway narrowed as the bridge ended and the town's main street began. Holiday had devoted the entirety of the flight researching the town of Alemos Island, but the internet photos didn't do justice to the quaint tableau before her. A cobblestone sidewalk edged a series of brick-and-stone storefronts, all centered around a tiny town square with a towering clapboard church and spire at the far end.

"Set design by Currier and Ives," Holiday murmured to herself as she eased into the first parking spot she saw. "Wardrobe by L.L. Bean."

According to GPS, she was a mere two-minute walk from Black Bear Bakery, purveyor of world-famous apple tarts that happened to be a favorite among locals in general and Alex Sappier in particular. Or so said their Instagram post from seven months ago.

Holiday had carefully considered the best method to approach and apprehend her target. She knew that Alex rarely left the island and that he owned and operated a small business with his younger brother. She'd considered calling ahead to make an appointment to speak with him at his office, but she didn't want this to feel business-y. Everything she'd read about him indicated that he was level-headed, methodical, and not prone to rash decisions. Which was why she had to ambush him, dazzle him with her charm offensive, and fast-talk him into agreeing to a blind date before he could come to his senses. Stun and run. Shock and awe.

She braced herself for the shock and awe of the Maine winter wind as she opened the car door and sprinted into the warm bakery, where she bought a trio of tarts and double-checked the location of the bar and grill where Alex routinely had lunch on Saturdays—thank you, social media accounts of the Wily Whale Coffee House and Tap Room.

After she stashed the baked goods in the back seat of the sedan, she swiped on some lipstick, recited a few calming mantras (useless, as usual), and prepared to secure her target.

Who was already striding past her car and heading toward the town square? Crap. He wasn't supposed to be here yet! How could the Wily Whale Facebook page mislead her so cruelly?

Holiday slammed out of her car and hurried down the street, waving and yelling at the two men about to round the corner.

"Hey! You!" She inwardly cringed. Talk about shock and awe.

The men stopped, turned around, and stared at her. As did all the pedestrians on the other side of the street.

"Hi!" She forced herself to lower her arm and her voice as she approached him. "Are you Alex Sappier?"

The men glanced at each other, then back at her. The taller one—who she knew perfectly well was Alex—said, "Maybe."

Holiday nodded and directed her attention to the second guy. "And you must be the brother. Pete, is it?"

The second guy glanced behind him, as though she might have been addressing someone else. "Paul."

So much for the charm offensive. She switched tactics to a more businesslike Q&A. "You two operate a charter plane business together, correct?"

Paul looked as though he was prepared to succumb to her interrogation, but Alex stepped in and cut him off. "Who are you?"

She tucked her hair behind her ear. "I'm Holiday Smith and I'm here with an amazing opportunity for you." She pulled out a business card and handed it to him.

He glanced at her name and job title and raised his eyebrows. "You're telling me that your job title is something called a 'Christmas Concierge' and that your name is Holiday?"

Holiday had variations of this conversation on a near-daily basis. "Yes, those are the facts." She shrugged. "Holiday is my legal, government name."

He looked less suspicious and more intrigued by the moment. "There's got to be a story there."

Holiday smiled as she thought of her family. "My mom was a huge Billie Holiday fan. My sister's name is Nora."

Both men regarded her blankly.

"Billie Holiday's real name was Eleanora Fagan. Mom took that theme and ran with it." She nodded down at the business card. "As I was saying, I'm Holiday Smith and I'm going to need you to come with me."

"Are we under arrest?" Paul looked excited.

"Not you." Holiday lifted her chin toward Alex. "Just him."

Paul glanced at his brother. "Call your attorney, dude."

"That won't be necessary," she assured him.

"That's what they all say until it's too late and you've incriminated yourself." Paul folded his arms over his heavy plaid jacket. "I've watched enough *Law & Order* to know how this works."

Alex was clearly trying to suppress a smile.

"I come bearing gifts." Holiday beckoned back them toward her car. "Apple tarts, fresh out of the oven at Black Bear Bakery."

"We're getting kidnapped for sure," Paul muttered.

Holiday opened the car door and handed them the bakery box tied with red twine. "Help yourself."

Paul wasted no time ripping off the string and seizing a tart. Alex hung back, observing and taking her measure.

"Have one of these." Paul practically shoved a tart into his brother's mouth. "They're delicious."

Alex pushed the pastry away. He continued to study Holiday with equal parts curiosity and suspicion. As the moments ticked by, Holiday started to understand why young Francie had harbored such a crush all those years. He was definitely the strong, silent type, but there was also a bright, playful glint in those dark-brown eyes. Even in a parka and jeans, he was a force to be reckoned with. She was willing to bet that he was quite good at . . . ahem . . . "reckoning," but right now, she needed to keep her mind out of the gutter and on the business matter at hand.

"Listen, Alex, I know that you're a busy, fiercely private individual." Holiday cleared her throat. "I also know—well, I heard—that you're single."

"Stalker with apple tarts," Paul mumbled through a mouthful of crumbs. "Score."

Holiday ignored him and waited for Alex to reply. He rocked back on his heels and took his time considering his response.

"What is it that you want from me, Ms. Smith?"

"Call me Holiday. And I don't want anything from you—I have a once-in-a-lifetime opportunity *for* you." Holiday pointed out the job title on her business card. "As a

Christmas concierge, I make people's wildest dreams come true. And I'm going to arrange a romantic evening with the woman of your dreams."

"That's it." He pulled out his phone. "I'm calling my attorney."

"Told ya," Paul said.

"Not so fast!" Holiday felt herself starting to sweat, despite the windchill. "Do you remember a girl from high school named Francie Penewate?"

Alex didn't even hesitate for a second. "Nope."

"She was a sophomore when you were a senior?" Holiday pressed. "Long dark hair, rosy cheeks, penchant for berets?"

"Doesn't ring a bell." But he slipped his phone back into his pocket.

Paul elbowed his brother. "Yes, it does. *Francie*, remember?"

He shook his head. "Clearly, I don't."

"She was hot," Paul said.

"Yes!" Holiday jabbed her index finger in victory. "Thank you, Paul. Francie was indeed hot. And guess what? She still is."

Paul leaned in. "Go on."

"Her grandmother—who is just the sweetest woman alive—would love it if Francie could find a smart, stable, kindhearted man such as yourself." She tilted her head at Alex and resumed Operation: Charm Offensive.

Alex folded his arms. "How do you know I'm not a soulless sociopath?"

"I ran multiple background checks, of course," Holiday

scoffed. "What is this, amateur hour?"

That faint, sexy smile reappeared. *Wait. No, no, no. Not sexy. Just . . . attractive. Alex was objectively, factually attractive, as was his smile.* She straightened her scarf as she tried to get back on track. "You're welcome to run a background check on me as well."

"That won't be necessary," he assured her. "Since this deal isn't going to get done."

"Let's not frame this as some sort of 'deal.'" She pulled up some photos of Francie. "It's your lucky day! I've compiled a dossier on this case and I can assure you that Francie is exceptionally bright, beautiful, classy and—"

"Nope." Alex started walking away. Paul followed, glancing back with every other step.

"Take a chance!" Holiday forced herself not to run after him. She stood her ground and made every effort to project confidence, even though she was shivering from the cold. "It's one date! What's the big deal?"

He stopped, but didn't turn around. "It's a big-enough deal that you trekked all the way out here from . . ."

"Virginia," she supplied.

He turned halfway. "Which tells me that you're highly motivated. Someone's paying you a lot of money to wrangle me into this."

"Ooh, like a bounty hunter!" Paul seemed delighted by the idea.

"Okay, let's go with that." Holiday shrugged. "I like to think of myself as Santa with better boots, but I could also be construed as a yuletide bounty hunter. And, Alex Sappier, you're the bounty."

Alex finally turned to face her. "How much is the price on my head?"

"Um, nothing, actually," Holiday conceded. "Just travel expenses. It's more of a matter of making up for past mistakes. I owe Francie's grandmother a favor, and this was her ask."

"Oof." Paul grimaced. "You're a charity case, man."

Alex looked like he was seconds away from smacking his brother. "If you did a background check, then you know that I used to work in big tech."

"Yeah, but I kind of skimmed over that part. Something about biomed technology?"

"I left that world because I didn't like all the pressure and manipulation. I refuse to be strong-armed into other people's agendas."

"Also, you made an obscene amount of money and could retire," Paul added.

Holiday knew that Alex had used a fraction of his fortune to stake the brothers' charter plane business. Paul flew the routes and chatted up the visitors while Alex oversaw the books and logistics. Alex Sappier was definitely not in need of any more money. So what else could she use to persuade him?

"No offense, but there's no upside for me in doing this deal." It was as if he'd read her mind.

She knew this was pathetic, but she had to try. "But it's Christmas. 'Tis the season of giving and doing for others."

He leveled his gaze at her. "You should be ashamed of

yourself."

"I am." She hung her head.

Alex shook his head. "We're done here. There's nothing on the table."

The brothers strode away, their footing sure and steady on the slick pavement.

"Hey!" she yelled after them. "I want my pastry back!"

Paul turned around, his face dusted with powdered sugar. "Too late. Sorry!"

And with that, they turned the corner and were gone.

Chapter Five

TWENTY MINUTES LATER, Holiday commandeered a corner booth at the Wily Whale Coffee House and Tap Room, ordered a café au lait, and tried to come up with a Plan B that would satisfy Mrs. Penewate and her grand-daughter.

She sipped her coffee, letting the warmth from the mug seep into her frozen fingers, and surveyed the crowd. The locals opted for warmth over style, for obvious reasons. It was wall-to-wall flannel, down parkas, and shearling caps with earflaps. A refreshing change from the logo-conscious, status-obsessed circles Holiday moved in. Alemos Island was simply too rugged and wild to be subject to the whims of fashion.

"How's your coffee, hon?" The server stopped by the table on her way to the kitchen.

"It's perfect, thank you." Holiday stared glumly into the warm, rich drink.

"You a friend of Alex's?" the server asked. She laughed when Holiday's head snapped up. "I noticed you were talking to him out there on the sidewalk. Well, actually, someone in the front booth noticed, and word traveled all the way back to the kitchen in two minutes."

"Wow."

"It's a long winter and we don't have much happening here on the island." The server plunked her tray down on the table and shifted her weight. "Sometimes it's deer season, sometimes it's grouse season . . . but it's *always* gossip season here."

Holiday glanced around the room and realized that the other customers and staff members were very studiously *not* looking her way. "And you got elected to get the scoop?"

The server winked. "I volunteered."

"Well, I hate to disappoint you, but I'm not a friend of Alex's." At this, the server looked even more intrigued, so Holiday hastened to add, "I just met him."

The server's eyes went wide. "So it's more of a fling?"

"No." Holiday had to laugh. "I came out here on business."

"Ooh, what kind of business?"

Holiday didn't have it in her to have the whole Christmas concierge conversation right now. "I'm not at liberty to say."

"Got it." The server nodded as if this explained everything. "You're in from Boston, right? One of the high-powered tech geniuses from his old life?"

"Um . . ."

"Well, it's too bad you're not a fling or a friend. We'd all like to see him find someone special. He's such a nice guy, you know? Really goes out of his way."

Holiday managed not to spit out her mouthful of coffee. "Um . . ."

"He practically rebuilt this town single-handedly. Getting all the roads repaved, renovating the school buildings . . ."

"It's nice that he's generous with his money," Holiday conceded.

"Oh, it's more than that! He was there in the elementary school along with the work crews, putting up drywall and swinging his hammer." The server picked up the tray and fanned her face. "It was a sight to behold, I can tell you."

"So people like him here?" Holiday furrowed her brow. "You find him helpful and nice?"

"He's the best!"

"Interesting." She picked up the coat lying on the bench next to her. "I'm ready for the check, please."

The server snapped out of her reverie. "Oh no, honey. Before you leave, you have to try our world-famous chowder."

"Thank you, but I really should go." Holiday nibbled her lower lip. "I have to make a phone call."

"Just a cup!" the server insisted. "It's my great-aunt's recipe. You're a friend of Alex, so it's on the house."

"I'm not . . ." Holiday trailed off when she registered the server's hopeful, helpful expression. "Yes, thank you. I'd love to try it."

While the server dashed back to the kitchen to deliver the nongossip and fetch the cup of chowder, Holiday pulled out her cell phone and stared at the hard, shiny screen. She was going to have to call Mrs. Penewate and deliver the news that she had failed to secure the target. She was going to have to disappoint one of her long-term clients—*again*—because Alex Sappier, the so-called nicest, most helpful fellow in existence, wouldn't agree to even sit down at the bargaining table with her. She was going to be the reason that Francie Penewate spent her Christmas alone instead of with the man of her dreams.

She was going to have to admit her failings and beg for forgiveness.

But first, chowder.

HOLIDAY WAS SPOONING up the last drops of the thick, creamy chowder and preparing to dial her cell phone when the bell above the front door jingled as Alex and Paul walked in. Alex had a black backpack in one hand and an unmistakable expression of guilt on his face.

Everyone in the restaurant swiveled their heads from Alex to Holiday to their dining companions. All the clattering cutlery stilled and an electrified hum of conversation buzzed through the dining room.

At first, Holiday wondered if this might be a small-town coincidence, if Alex and his brother had no idea that she was still in Alemos, let alone their favorite lunch spot. But then his gaze locked on to her, and there was no mistaking his look of purpose.

He was coming back to the bargaining table. Literally and metaphorically.

As the brothers approached, Holiday nodded to the

bench opposite hers, indicating that they should sit down.

As Alex and Paul slid into the booth, the server practical-ly knocked over a busboy in her haste to get to the table.

"Look who's here!" she trilled.

"Hi, Sally," Alex and Paul chorused.

Sally whirled to face Holiday, who smiled and said noth-ing.

When the silence at the table stretched into an awkward pause, Sally flipped her ponytail and nodded at Paul, then Alex. "You boys want your usual?"

"Yes, thanks." Alex waited until Sally was out of earshot, then unzipped the backpack and regarded Holiday with a look of resignation.

"We're back," he announced.

"I can see that." She stacked one hand atop the other and prepared to negotiate. "It's good to see you again."

Alex sighed. "Remember how I said there's nothing on the table?"

She nodded. "I do."

"And how I hate being pressured and manipulated?"

"Mm-hmm."

A brief, silent scuffle broke out between brothers as Alex and Paul kicked each other beneath the table.

Holiday made a big show of checking her watch. "Gen-tlemen. How may I be of service?"

Alex drew a deep breath and shot Paul an absolutely deadly glare. "You said you can find anything? Absolutely anything?"

Her adrenaline surged. "If it exists in time and space, I

can find it."

The brothers exchanged another round of furious glances, and she knew she had him. *One burly, bitter ex–tech bro in the bag.*

Alex settled into his own negotiation posture. "Are you familiar with Driscoll Davidson?"

"The stained-glass guy? Of course." Holiday had seen a traveling exhibition of Davidson's colorful window panels and lamps a few years ago at the Metropolitan Museum of Art.

"Did you know that he grew up in Maine?"

"No." She glanced at the backpack. "What's in there?"

"Did you know that, back before he became famous and successful, Driscoll Davidson used to make Christmas ornaments?"

"No. That's so cool!"

"Not really." Paul looked to be on the verge of tears.

"Let me do the talking," Alex muttered. He turned his attention back to Holiday. "When my parents got married, they got a Driscoll Davidson Christmas tree star as a wedding present. Rich uncle or something. I don't know the details."

"And it's ruined," Paul blurted out. "We ruined it."

"I *said*, let me do the talking." Alex unzipped the backpack. "There was a mishap."

He handed the backpack to Holiday, who peered inside at a pile of broken glass shards and the remnants of a bronze star outline. "Holy smithereens, Batman. Is this . . .?"

"It was," Alex confirmed.

She couldn't conceal her dismay as she regarded the wreckage that had once been a historic, handcrafted—not to mention priceless—tree topper. "What did you *do*?"

"He did it." Alex and Paul spoke simultaneously and pointed at each other.

She picked up a single jagged shard of red glass. "You guys are going to art history hell."

"Obviously, it was an accident," Alex said.

"Yeah." Paul took a grateful gulp as the server arrived with two pints of beers. "A really, really unfortunate accident."

"We just started to decorate my mom's house for Christmas," Alex explained. "My dad died a few months ago and my mom can't drag out the tree and all the heavy boxes of decorations by herself. So, we waited until she went out this morning and then got everything ready to surprise her."

"The stockings, the nativity scene, everything." Paul closed his eyes, imagining the scene of the crime.

"Which is why I was so short with you when you flagged me down on the street," Alex added.

Holiday inclined her head. "Continue."

"We put all the ornaments on the tree—"

"Exactly evenly spaced," Paul murmured. "Because somebody is compulsive."

"I like radial symmetry," Alex shot back. "So does nature."

"He used a *tape measure*," Paul told Holiday. "For ornaments."

"Everything was exactly right," Alex finished. "And then

we got out the ladder to put the star on the tree and . . . mistakes were made."

Holiday peered into the sack full of shards. "Is your mother upset?"

"She will be if she ever finds out," Alex said. "But she won't, if you're half the Christmas concierge you claim to be."

Holiday zipped up the backpack and signaled to Sally. "I'm going to need more caffeine, please."

Chapter Six

"**I**'M NOT SURE you appreciate the magnitude of this situation." Holiday gratefully acceptedthe café au lait Sally delivered to the table, along with two beers for the Sappier brothers. "There's only four days until Christmas."

"You said you could find anything, anytime, anyplace," Alex reminded her, raising his pint glass in homage.

"Yeah, assuming it's findable!" Holiday's palms started to sweat. "But an original antique Driscoll Davidson star with red accents?"

Paul peeked back into the backpack. "Red and gold, actually."

Holiday knew she should say no. She had learned the hard way what happened when she overestimated her own capabilities. Yet when she opened her mouth, she found herself asking, "Do you have a photo of what the original looked like?"

"Lots," Alex assured her.

"And, I mean, not to insult your legendary genius or whatever, but have you tried eBay?"

"I'm going to pretend you didn't ask that." He looked affronted. "Of course I tried eBay. I checked a dozen online auction sites."

She held up one hand. "Okay, I get it."

"And what I found out is, everyone wants to *buy* a star like this, but no one wants to *sell* them." The bench creaked as Alex settled back. "This, Holiday Smith, is your mission, should you choose to accept it."

Paul started humming the *Mission: Impossible* theme song.

"Can't you ask for something easier?" Holiday said. "Like finding Bigfoot or catching a leprechaun?"

"Leprechauns are out of season," Paul pointed out. "And we're in Maine. You'll definitely have a better chance with Bigfoot."

"This star is what I need." Alex locked his gaze with hers. "And Christmas is when I need it by."

"All right. Let's just assume I hunt it down for you," Holiday said. "Are you prepared to pay what this star is going to cost on the open market?"

"Yes." He didn't hesitate. "Price is not an issue. I'll pay anything. I'll *do* anything. I'll beg your forgiveness for blowing you off earlier."

"That won't be necessary," she assured him.

He seemed surprised. "It won't?"

"Of course not. I'm on a tight timeline and I don't have time for groveling."

He looked at her with newfound respect.

"But let's be clear: if I come through with this by Christmas, you'll go on the date with Francie?" She leveled her gaze at him.

Alex hesitated for a fraction of a second, during which

Paul assured Holiday, "He'll do it with a smile on his face and a song in his heart."

Holiday kept looking at Alex. "You will?"

He nodded. "I'm a man of my word."

"Okay, but you don't have a smile on your face," she informed him. "That's more of a grimace."

"I'll be smiling when the deal's done," he vowed.

"Give me two minutes." Holiday dashed out the door of the coffee shop, turned her back to the frigid wind, and dialed her sister's number.

Nora picked up on the third ring. "How's the tundra?"

"You know, it's not that cold once you lose all feeling in your limbs," Holiday replied.

"Way to look on the bright side. Next thing we know, you'll be doing the polar bear swim on New Year's Day."

Holiday shivered, sought shelter under a storefront awning, and got to the point. "I'm calling with a long-overdue apology."

"Really?" Nora started laughing. "Is the apocalypse here already?"

"Remember how, when you said you were going to major in art history, I made fun of you and said you would live in Mom and Dad's basement until you were thirty-five?"

"Yes, I do."

"And you said that someday I'd be sorry and come crawling to you for help?"

"Yessss." Nora's voice lilted.

"Well, today's the day." Holiday summarized the stained glass star situation as quickly as possible. "I need your art

history contacts. Auction house employees, museum cura-
tors, gallery owners, glasswork collectors."

"This isn't like you," Nora said. "You sound panicked."

"I'm not panicked, I'm . . . yeah, okay, I'm panicked."

"This Alex guy sounds like a pain in the butt."

"Truer words were never spoken. But these are the terms
of the deal. It's pay-to-play with a Driscoll Davidson star,
circa 1980, that may not even exist."

"Is he good-looking, at least?" Nora pressed. "It's easier
to deal with annoying men when they're good-looking."

"He's all right, if you like tall, athletic guys with five-
o'clock shadows and a closet full of wool sweaters."

"Ooh, go on."

"His looks are not the issue here," Holiday said. "He's
just a means to an end. I have to bend him to my will so I
can A, redeem my flawless track record, and B, walk through
Mom and Dad's door before dawn on Christmas morning."

"Oh, honey." Nora's voice turned wistful. "You're not
still telling yourself you'll be home for Christmas, are you?"

"You'll see!" Holiday hopped a few times for emphasis.
And to warm herself up. "I'll be right in your face on
Christmas morning, and I will say, 'I told you so,' and *you*
will be the one who has to apologize then!"

"Uh-huh. What's the deadline for finding this mythical
tree topper?"

"Last week would be ideal."

"Guess I better start making some calls. Tell you what,
I'll try to find you a time machine while I'm at it."

"You're the best sister ever."

"Actual and factual."

"See you Christmas morning." Holiday huddled deeper into her jacket and started toward the entrance to the coffee shop.

Nora sighed. "Let's focus on one miracle at a time, shall we?"

Holiday strode back into the Wily Whale with swagger to spare. Alex glanced up from his beer and, for the first time since she'd met him, looked a little unsure of himself.

As he should be. The gloves are coming off. Literally. She peeled off her fleece-lined mittens as she approached the table.

"Your coffee's getting cold," Paul said.

"Doesn't matter. I won't have time to finish it. I've got things to do and people to see."

The two brothers exchanged a glance. "Do you have a lead?"

"All in good time, fellas." She tossed some cash down on the table. "Drinks are on me. And Alex?"

He went a bit pale beneath that rugged stubble on his cheeks. "Yeah?"

"You better break out your cologne and start chilling champagne, because you're going to be the dreamiest dream date this side of the Arctic Circle come Christmas Eve."

HOLIDAY CURSED THE rental car company as the sedan skidded on a patch of ice when she turned into the parking lot for the Alemos Island Inn. The old Victorian mansion was draped with twinkle lights and green garlands in honor of the Christmas season. When Holiday had visited the inn's website, she'd discovered that the hotel hosted multiple gingerbread competitions. The inn itself resembled an ornate cookie construction, with spindly porch railings, steep gables, and copper rooftop finials. The white-and-green structure managed to look quaint and grand simultaneously.

I just hope they have central heating. She wrestled her suitcase out of the trunk and wheeled it across the salt-strewn path to the porch stairs. When she reached the reception desk, the air was still chilly enough to see her breath.

"Good afternoon, dear." The grandmotherly innkeeper garbed in a white turtleneck and a chic red leather jacket greeted her from the registration desk. "Would you care for a piece of shortbread?"

"Always." Holiday helped herself to a square. "Mmm, this is divine."

"My husband bakes them from scratch every other day."

Holiday closed her eyes and savored the buttery crumbles. "I need to find a husband like that."

"Are you checking in?" The innkeeper hauled out a leather-bound ledger and flipped through the pages.

Holiday provided her name and reservation number.

The innkeeper ran her index finger down a column of handwritten names. "Ah yes, I have you down for the turret room. I hope you like pink chintz."

"You know what I like? Heat."

"We just replaced the heating system last year. I think

you'll be quite comfortable."

"And is there a shower with lots of hot water?"

"Yes, there is. I'm Michelina and I'm going to make sure you have a lovely stay with us stay until you check out on the . . ." She peered at the ledger.

"Twenty-fourth," Holiday supplied. "Going home for Christmas."

"Wonderful. Do you need help with your bags?"

"No, thank you. But I do need the Wi-Fi password."

"I'm afraid our Wi-Fi is down at the moment and cellular service is spotty all over the island. Hence, the handwritten reservations." Michelina chuckled at Holiday's horrified expression. "Not to worry, if you're truly desperate, one of our guests managed to get cell service on the back porch a few days ago."

"Like, outside?"

"Well, yes, technically, but there's an overhang."

Holiday hesitated for a moment, considering her options. Cell service was essential to her current quest, but moving to another hotel would be tricky, if not impossible, on such short notice. For one thing, most of the local hotels were already booked to capacity with seasonal guests. For another thing, changing hotels would mean going back outside, turning on her car and shivering while she waited for the heater to kick in, and fishtailing down the ice-slick roads.

"And, of course, you're welcome to go to the public library or the little wine bar down the street for Wi-Fi."

"Books and wine? I'll make it work," she assured Michelina.

"Here, take another piece of shortbread," Michelina urged. "Tea time is four o'clock sharp."

"Does your husband bake for that too?"

"He does. I believe he's making cranberry scones today."

"See you at four." Dragging her suitcase up the series of narrow, carpeted stairs was enough to count as Holiday's cardio and weight training of the day. "Save me a scone."

MICHELINA HAD NOT been kidding about the pink chintz. The guest room in the turret looked as though it had been sponsored by Pepto Bismol and decorated by Barbie. A canopied four-poster bed draped in rose-patterned fabric backed up to pink damask wallpaper. The rug featured pink flowers woven into a mint-green background and the pink sofa in the corner was ruffled, tufted, and heaped with pastel throw pillows. Holiday felt certain that when she turned off the lights tonight, she would still be able to *hear* pink.

But no matter. The shower—tiled in a daring shade of salmon—featured hot water. Holiday turned the bathroom's space heater up to full blast, then stood under the shower until her toes and fingertips no longer felt tingly and chilled. She allowed herself five minutes of indulgence, then turned off the shower, dried off in a huge fluffy towel—fuchsia— and pulled on wool socks, long underwear, fleece-lined jeans, and a cashmere sweater before donning boots and her parka. She paused to examine her reflection in the mirror on her way out the door. The ensemble was missing something . . . like a down-filled sleeping bag or a heating pad in each pocket.

But this would have to do for now. She navigated the stairs with care, her mobility significantly limited by all the layers, and decided that she was ready to brave the back porch. She slipped off her gloves, held up her cell phone, and braced herself for the arctic blast as she opened the inn's back door.

Thirty seconds later, she abandoned the whole "arctic blast" plan and power walked down the street to the public library, thinking toasty warm thoughts all the way.

The Alemos Island library looked like a rustic little cabin nestled behind a copse of fir trees and a weathered bronze statue of a moose. Holiday noted the library's hours as she opened the glass-paned door and figured she had thirty minutes—forty-five, tops—to make calls and browse the internet until the powers that be kicked her out. She paused on the threshold to close her eyes and inhale that distinct *eau de bibliotechque*—a mélange of yellowing pages, ballpoint pen ink, and graham cracker crumbs ground into the rug in the children's section. But this heady perfume was cut with the sharp scent of dark-roast espresso.

Holiday glanced at the circulation desk, where the librarian on duty was sipping from a double-walled glass cup. The librarian nodded at Holiday, who nodded back and glanced at the clock above the "New Arrivals" shelf.

"I'll only be a few minutes," Holiday murmured. She headed for the computer carrels, peeled off the first few layers of outerwear, settled in behind the keyboard, and prepared to launch into a lightning-round search session for "Driscoll Davidson."

And yet . . . somehow her fingers, entirely of their own accord, typed "Alexander Sappier" into the search engine. And then, instead of reading any of the articles that summarized his academic prowess and career achievements, she found herself clicking on "Images," which produced dozens of photos of Francie Penewate's future dream date. Behold, Alex in a board meeting. Alex giving a commencement speech. Alex wearing a tux at a fundraising event.

Wow. And she'd thought the man had looked good in a sweater.

"Is that Alex Sappier?" a voice behind her asked.

Holiday had a heart attack, died, and came back to life in the span of three seconds. Gasping, she whirled around in her chair to face the librarian from the front desk.

"Sorry, didn't mean to startle you." The woman nodded down at her high-top sneakers. "Ever since we installed the new carpeting, I keep sneaking up on people by accident."

"That's okay." Holiday realized that she still had one hand pressed to her chest.

The librarian focused on the computer screen. "It's ludicrous, right? That one guy gets to be that smart and that successful and that good-looking? In what world is that fair?"

Holiday felt heat seeping into her cheeks as she clicked the browser window closed. "Oh, I was just, um . . ."

"No need to explain. Your web searches are your business." The librarian grinned and extended her right hand.

"I'm Janine. Can I help you find anything?"

Holiday shook hands and turned back to the computer screen. "No, thank you. I'm staying at the inn down the street and the Wi-Fi's out."

"Got it. Well, I'm here if you need me. And if you'd like some book recommendations, there are some great historical romances over there." Janine pointed to the next room. "Some of the cover models kind of look like Alex, actually."

Holiday's voice rose an octave. "Great, thanks, bye." Suffused in self-consciousness, she retreated to the farthest corner of the children's area, where she found a window seat adorned with a stuffed Eeyore and Winnie the Pooh. She dialed her sister's number and asked Nora if she'd discovered anything new about Driscoll Davidson pieces.

"No, I have not" was Nora's crisp response. "It's only been an hour since the last time you asked me and everyone is out of the office for Christmas."

"But it's an art history emergency," Holiday said.

"For you. Everyone else is panicking about how to cook a turkey and where to buy a last-minute gift for their uncle."

"Slackers," Holidays murmured.

"We don't all focus on Christmas twelve months year," Nora said. "Everyone deserves a vacation." She paused. "Even the Christmas concierge."

"I said I'll be home," Holiday rage-whispered.

"And I said I'll believe it when I see it," Nora rage-whispered right back. "I'd help you with Driscoll Davidson if I could, but honestly? I'd be surprised if anyone called me back before January."

"But—"

"Holiday, I love you, but you need to know when to quit."

"The Wish Granter never quits." Holiday picked up Eeyore in solidarity.

"And, at a certain point, you might want to ask yourself, 'Is that really a good thing?'"

"It's neither good nor bad. It just is." She clicked off her phone, stood up from the window seat, and nearly ran into Janine. "Whoa. Hi again."

"Hi." Janine still had her espresso mug in hand. "I couldn't help overhearing that you're looking for information about Driscoll Davidson."

Holiday glanced down at her phone. "Am I that loud?"

"No, this time I was just blatantly eavesdropping." Janine repositioned a displayed copy of *The Very Hungry Caterpillar*. "But the good news is, I might be able to help you."

"No offense, but I doubt it."

"Try me. In addition to being very nosy, I'm also very knowledgeable."

"Long story short, I'm looking for a vintage stained-glass Christmas tree topper from Driscoll Davidson's studio and there's nothing available online, and all the art people and auctioneers who might be able to track something down are on vacation." Holiday was starting to relate to Eeyore on multiple levels. "It's time-sensitive."

Janine put down her espresso cup. "Have you talked to his family members?"

"Driscoll Davidson's? No."

"You do know that he used to spend his summers on the coast of Maine, right? And that he had a bunch of kids, some of whom inherited and ran his studio after he died?" Janine motioned her in. "And that there were some big family feuds, and that many of the grandchildren and great-grandchildren are rumored to have made off with early, valuable pieces and have them stashed away in undisclosed locations? And that it's all very dramatic and scandalous, like a stained-glass soap opera?"

"I did not know that." Holiday stood up and squared her shoulders. "But I'm guessing that I don't need to, because you miraculously know the names, addresses, and social security numbers of all his descendants?"

Janine laughed. "Even I'm not that nosy. But you don't need a miracle. All you need is a good genealogy chart, and we do have that." She turned and headed back toward the circulation desk. "Follow me."

"Are you sure? I don't want to keep you past closing time."

"Closing time is when I say it is," Janine assured her. "Hang on, let me find the keys to the basement. That's where we keep all the rare documents and town history artifacts."

"If I'm going with you to a creepy storage room in a basement, I should probably introduce myself. I'm Holiday Smith and I'm a Christmas concierge."

Janine accepted both the name and the job title without missing a beat. "Pleased to meet you. And don't worry, the basement is one hundred percent well-lit and noncreepy."

Indeed, the storage room turned out to be a moisture-controlled vault with overhead fluorescent lighting so bright, Holiday felt like she should have sunscreen. While her pupils were still adjusting, Janine was already opening drawers and unrolling scrolls.

"Let's see . . . I think the original documents would be from the 1940s." Janine crouched down to rummage through the lowest drawer of a battered metal cabinet. She hummed a little tune while rifling through yellowing documents with dizzying speed. After a few minutes, she extracted a large rectangle of paper from the drawers. "Here we go." She placed the wafer-thin document on the table in the middle of the room and ran her index finger over the fading black ink.

"Okay, we start up here with Anne and Calvin Davidson, who were Driscoll's parents." Janine stepped to one side so that Holiday could follow along as she traced the lineages. "Here's Driscoll and his wife, Rose."

"This is amazing." Holiday ran her fingertips over the smooth, fragile paper. "I feel like I'm in a PBS documentary."

Janine's indulgent smile morphed into a creased brow. "Uh-oh."

"What?" Holiday strained to see the source of the librarian's distress.

"So apparently, the family feud got even feud-ier than I thought." Janine pointed out a series of angry black scratch marks under Driscoll's branch of the family tree. "Some philistine defaced this."

Holiday's hope deflated as the ramifications of this registered. "And now we can't read the names of the relatives who probably have the lost stash of glass?"

"I can't believe this." Janine staggered back as if she'd been physically wounded. "These are irreplaceable historical documents. To just take a *Sharpie* to them . . ."

"Someone was serious about erasing half of the family tree."

"Then they should have sued each other or fought it out bare-knuckled in the street! Don't bring your petty nonsense into the library." Janine looked to be on the verge of tears.

"We'll find the culprits," Holiday vowed.

"But how? Someone heartless and deviant enough to do this probably crossed out their own name in addition to everyone else's. And now we're missing information going back at least two generations . . ."

Holiday clapped her hands together. "That's it! That's how we find them."

"Who?"

"The missing relatives, the missing glass pieces, everything." She started pacing around the vault in her excitement. "We look for them the same way the cops look for serial killers."

Janine scoffed. "Listen, I have a lot of pull in this town, but there's no way the police department is going to put a task force together to track down a genealogy vandal from twenty years ago."

"We can do it ourselves. All we need is some spit in a cup." Holiday laughed at Janine's expression. "An at-home

DNA testing kit. That's how they solve a lot of cold cases now. All we need is the name and address of one of the relatives whose name is still legible."

"And then what? Show up on their doorstep and ask if we can swab their cheek?" Janine sounded doubtful.

"I'll take care of that part," Holiday assured her. "You're very knowledgeable. I'm very persuasive."

Janine shook her head. "Yeah, but even if you lucked out and got a hit for a bunch of Davidson relatives, you'd never get the results back before Christmas."

"You're right," Holiday allowed. "*I* wouldn't. But I know a guy with connections in the biotech world."

Chapter Seven

"CONGRATULATIONS, YOU REELED me in with your cryptic text. I'm here." Alex strode into the sitting room of the Alemos Island Inn looking like a chisel-jawed J. Crew model in a marled gray sweater and faded jeans.

Holiday—along with several other female guests milling around the fireplace—turned to admire the view. "Oh, good. I wasn't sure if you replied, given the tragic lack of cell service here."

"I didn't reply. There's no appropriate response to a text like that." He glanced down at his cell phone to read her own words back to her: "*SOS. Stained-glass summit meeting urgently requested. Meet at the inn at 4 p.m. sharp.*"

"Sit down." Holiday gestured to a red-and-white-striped sofa by the ten-foot-tall Christmas tree. "Have a scone . . . they're perfection. And then, prepare to be dazzled by my brilliance."

"Stained-glass summit first, scones second."

"Have it your way." Holiday sat down and clasped her hands in her lap. "I'm trying to track down some estranged relatives of Driscoll Davidson. Rumor has it that they may have a secret stash of stained-glass pieces that have never gone out on the market due to squabbling and spite."

He shook his head. "'Trying' doesn't work for me. My mother asked about the whereabouts of her tree topper the second she came home and saw the other decorations. I'm making excuses about having accidentally moved some her boxes into my garage, but that's not going to hold her off for much longer."

"Time is of the essence," Holiday agreed. "Which brings us to the crucial question: Do you still have pull in the biotech world?"

His eyes narrowed in suspicion. "I'm going to need more details."

Holiday gave him a thirty-second rundown of the genealogy vandal. "So I'm going to get a saliva sample from one of the known relatives in order to fill in some of the gaps on the family tree."

"Like how they found the Golden State killer?"

"Exactly! But with stained glass instead of murder."

His suspicion turned into skepticism. "How are you planning to get the saliva sample?"

She waved away this little detail. "You needn't concern yourself with that. The more pressing question is, how do I get the DNA results back in time to track down the other relatives by Christmas?"

"You need to fast-track the test results," he concluded.

"Yeah. Like, particle-accelerator speed." She crossed her fingers and sucked in her breath. "What do you think?"

He settled back into the green velvet throw pillows and let her suffer in anticipation for a few seconds.

"Well?" she prompted.

That slow, smoldering half smile reappeared. "I think you're incredibly lucky to know one of the original investors of a DIY DNA kit."

She actually bounced up and down on the couch. "Victory! Fantastic. How long do you think turnaround time will be?"

He gazed upward, doing the calculations in his head. "You give me the sample. I'll have Paul fly it to the mainland, then the company jet flies it to the lab . . . twelve hours? Fifteen?"

She had to restrain herself from punching the air *à la* Rocky atop the stone steps. "Yes! We are totally gonna get this done."

On impulse, she opened her arms for a hug. He leaned in for the hug. Both of them froze, mere inches apart.

She pulled back, smoothing the front of her sweater. "So. Great. Okay."

He tugged at the collar of his sweater. "Okay."

As they retreated to their separate corners of the couch, an attractive woman in an ecru sweater dress and fur-trimmed boots approached. "Excuse me." She pointed first at Alex, then at Holiday. "Are you two together?"

Holiday brushed her hair back from her face in what was meant to be a casual gesture and ended up getting a strand tangled in her eyelashes. "Us?" She blinked furiously. "No."

The woman turned to Alex, one eyebrow raised.

"No, we're not together." He cleared his throat. "We're, um, business partners."

"Oh, good." She smiled at Alex. "Then would you like to

walk over to the wine bar and have a drink with me?"

Before Alex could open his mouth to reply, Holiday interjected. "He can't. He's taken."

Alex frowned at her. "I am not."

"Yes, you are," she hissed. "You're on hold for you-know-who."

"Figures." The woman sighed and nodded. "All the good ones are taken."

"You can't put me on hold." Alex stood up and gazed down at her. "I'm not a library book."

"You put yourself on hold," Holiday informed him. "When we agreed to terms at the Wily Whale. You're reserved until December twenty-sixth, buddy. Deal with it."

The attractive stranger sat down in a nearby armchair, apparently fascinated by this conversation.

Alex leveled an index finger at Holiday. "My reserve status depends on what happens with the saliva sample."

"Oh, I'm getting that saliva sample." Holiday yanked at the strand of hair, which was still in her eyes.

"We'll see. So far, you're all talk and no action." He turned to the lady in the sweater dress. "I would love to go have a glass of wine with you."

The woman held up her palm. "Never mind. I don't want to get in the way of whatever's going on here."

"Nothing's going on," Alex and Holiday said simultaneously.

"Uh-huh." She got to her feet and headed toward the fireplace. "I'm going to find a scone. You two enjoy your evening." As soon as she rejoined her friends, they all started whispering and glancing at Alex and Holiday.

Alex groaned. "We're going to be the talk of the town."

"Fine by me. I don't live here." Holiday grinned.

Alex hesitated for a moment, looked down, and then looked up at her again. "Since everyone's already gossiping, you want to go grab dinner at the wine bar?"

Yes. The certainty and immediacy of her response startled her. She forced herself to stop before blurting it out. Instead, she said, "I should probably just turn in for the night. I've been traveling all day and I have to get up at the crack of dawn to launch Operation Expectorate."

"Are you sure?" His irresistible smile reappeared. "They have baked brie."

Holiday forced herself to shake her head.

He leaned down to murmur in her ear, "Charcuterie boards."

She closed her eyes and promised herself she wouldn't cry until she got back to her room. "I can't."

He straightened up, undeterred. "Okay. Then I'll get takeout and leave it at the front desk for you."

"Oh, you don't—"

"I'm doing it," he informed her. "It's in my best interests. You need to keep your strength up for your big quest tomorrow. Grilled cheese and tomato soup sound good?"

"It sounds heavenly," she confessed.

"Great. I'll have them bring the food up to your room when it's ready."

Holiday had to take a moment to tamp down the hope and excitement whirling inside her. She reminded herself that she had come here with a specific goal and that falling for this guy was in direct conflict with the desired outcome. Then she forced herself to review her personal history, which offered overwhelming evidence that Yuletide romances didn't work out because December twenty-fifth was to her as April fifteenth was to an accountant. "Alex. This is really nice of you."

He shrugged. "Maybe that's why people I don't remember from high school still want to date me."

Holiday laughed. "Between that and your superior stained-glass-handling skills, how could anyone resist?"

"No one's perfect." He rolled his eyes. "And Holiday?"

"Yes?" She gazed up at him.

"If anyone can sweet-talk strangers into handing over their DNA, it's you."

HOLIDAY SLEPT SOUNDLY in her Fifty Shades of Pink suite. The grilled cheese and tomato soup had been the perfect comfort food after the long day of travel, and she'd drifted off before nine p.m., feeling cozy and calm.

Alex Sappier had turned out to be a lot more interesting than she'd expected. Plus more fun. If only circumstances were different . . . but they weren't. She was the Wish Granter, and she would grant Mrs. Penewate's wish regardless of her own desires.

After layering up in silk, cotton, and wool the next morning, she helped herself to a croissant and a cup of coffee from the old-timey carafe in the parlor—while assiduously avoiding eye contact with the female guest who'd tried to ask Alex out last night—and hurried down the street to the library to begin the search for the nearest Davidson relative's name and address.

The morning was breezy and a scattering of clouds blocked the sun. A light sprinkling of snow started to fall as she walked. Holiday prayed that the clear weather would hold and quickened her pace.

Upon arriving at the library doors, she discovered that building was closed until noon because it was Saturday. Undeterred, she huddled under the eaves and tried to access the library's Wi-Fi via her cell phone. By referencing the photos she had taken of the defaced family tree, Holiday determined that the nearest known descendant of Driscoll Davidson was a Pamela Donovan, age forty-four, who (per the internet) resided in a tiny town near Augusta, Maine. If there was no bridge traffic—and, realistically, there never seemed to be any traffic around here—the drive shouldn't take more than a few hours.

As Holiday stashed her phone back in her coat pocket, Janine bounded up the library steps, sure-footed in her canvas high-tops, despite the ice patches on the concrete. She greeted Holiday with a jaunty wave. "Morning, camper. You're a little early."

Holiday glanced back at the business hours posted on the door. "So are you. What are you doing here?"

"Oh, I always come in first thing to use the coffee maker. It's way better than the one I have at home. What are *you* doing here?"

"Still no Wi-Fi at the hotel. I'm freeloading yours," Holiday explained.

Janine smiled slyly. "Alex Sappier wouldn't let you use his? I heard you two were looking all holly-jolly yesterday."

Holiday's jaw dropped. "Are you kidding me?"

"That's the rumor going around."

"The lady at the Wily Whale said that gossip traveled fast, but that was only twelve hours ago!"

Janine laughed. "You guys'll probably be the top story on tonight's local newscast."

Holiday cringed. "We barely even touched!"

"To paraphrase Mark Twain, we don't let the truth get in the way of a good story." Janine jangled her keyring. "Besides, you two would make the cutest couple."

"No, no, no." Holiday blanched. "Don't even joke about that."

"I'm one hundred percent serious," Janine said.

"I can't poach my client's gift for her granddaughter. That's an ethics violation of the Christmas Concierge code. Not to mention extremely bad manners."

Janine started singing, "How can something so wrong . . . feel so right?"

"Not helping." Holiday inhaled deeply and took a moment to collect herself. "You know what? This conversation is over. I'm getting back into my car and driving to Augusta. I bid you good day, madam." She clutched the handrailing of the steps and tried not to fall. "PS, these stairs are a lawsuit waiting to happen."

"Don't worry, the city will sand the walkway before the library actually opens . . . in *four hours*." Janine's voice was right behind her. "What's in Augusta? Is this about the document-destroying delinquent?"

"Yep. I'm hoping to come back with a few strands of DNA. Wish me luck."

"I'm coming with you." Janine fell into step next to Holiday as she headed into the parking lot.

"Um . . . no, thank you."

"I'd like a few words with whoever vandalized a publicly owned historic document."

"That's counter to my purposes," Holiday pointed out. "I have to cajole this woman to part with her bodily fluids."

"Okay, so you do your thing first, and then turn her over to me."

"Eh . . ." Holiday pretended to consider this. "Pass." She walked to her rental car and spoke in a friendly but firm tone. "Thanks again for your help yesterday. I'll see you later."

Janine's eyebrows shot up. "That's your car?"

Holiday nodded.

"Have you checked the weather forecast?" Before Holiday could reply, Janine hustled her over to a rusty, weather-beaten Jeep. "Friends don't let friends drive on those tires in December. Hop in."

Holiday glanced back at the sedan, the windshield of which was already accumulating snow. "But . . ."

Janine hopped into the driver's seat, revved her engine, and rolled down the window. "Get in, city girl. You're welcome in advance."

Chapter Eight

"SO TELL ME." Janine turned the heater up and the car radio down as the Jeep merged onto the main highway. "How does one become a Christmas concierge?"

"Kind of by accident." Holiday unwound the merino wool scarf from around her neck as the warm air gusted in. "I was never really sure what I wanted to do when I grew up. You know how some kids know coming out of the womb that they want to be a doctor? A ballerina? A detective?"

"A librarian?" Janine patted her chest.

"Exactly. I never had that. I kind of be-bopped along, did fine in school, played lots of different sports, whatever. And then one day, in eighth grade—I still remember like it was yesterday—Mrs. Adelman announced we were going to do a scavenger hunt."

"God bless eighth-grade teachers."

"Totally." Holiday smiled at the memory. "I was a shrimp, one of the youngest and smallest kids in my class, but I decided that just as soon as Mrs. Adelman told us what the heck a scavenger hunt was, I was going to win it all."

"And did you?"

"Yep. I was racing around, snatching the slips of paper out of logs and tree stumps, figuring out the clues like that guy staring at the blackboard in *Good Will Hunting*. I was unstoppable."

"Did you get a prize?" Janine asked.

"No! I got yelled at by Mrs. Adelson for 'not showing good teamwork.'" Holiday still smarted at the memory. "And when I went home, I got yelled at by my mom for ripping my new pants while I was crawling on gravel trying to find a clue."

"The road to glory can be rocky."

"It was such a thrill, being able to find what no one else could find. Being able to put the pieces together and solve a puzzle." Holiday relaxed into the Jeep's heated passenger seat. "Also, most of my clients are filthy rich and spending other people's money is fun."

"I can only imagine."

"The Christmas gift stuff started with my grandmother," Holiday continued. "She used to give the most thoughtful presents. When she got older, she had trouble leaving her home, and the internet wasn't her wheelhouse. So, the day after Thanksgiving, I'd go to her house, drink peppermint cocoa with a metric ton of mini-marshmallows, and we'd brainstorm together. She'd walk me through the process of figuring out what different people would like, and then I'd scour the world wide web 'til I found it." Holiday smiled at the memory. "She was so thoughtful. And then word started to get around her canasta group, and pretty soon, half the population of the Elmsbrook senior center was asking me to help them track down the 'it' item of the year." She ticked off the various victories on her fingers. "Magic Mixies,

American Girl dolls, PlayStations. I was basically doing hand-to-hand combat at the loading docks of Toys"R"Us. At first it was fun, playing Santa's helper. I love traveling, seeing the world. Every day is a new adventure."

"The sights you must have seen," Janine mused.

"I've been everywhere from Miami to Mongolia. And I really get to make a difference in people's lives." Holiday surprised herself by tearing up a bit. "One woman wanted to find a rare baseball card for her husband, who was slowly losing his memory. Apparently, he'd had been looking for this particular card since he was a little kid. They had a big chunk of money set aside for traveling, but he couldn't travel anymore. She said she'd spend it all on that card if she needed to."

"Did you find it?"

"I sure did. Signed rookie card. I had it authenticated and mounted in a special case and everything. The woman and her husband were both so happy when he opened it on Christmas morning." Holiday had to clear her throat. "Dora, that was her name. Dora Kistler. She said he kept it on his nightstand and was always so thrilled to see it and talk about it, even after the dementia got really bad."

"Don't make me cry. I'm driving."

"And that was it. I was hooked. I had a lawyer draw up some documents, established an LLC and a commission structure, and hoped for the best." She shrugged. "It's been bananas ever since."

"Do you do any advertising?"

"None. No social media, either. Most of my referrals are

through word of mouth, and my customers don't want their personal business splashed all over Instagram."

"So how far in advance do customers need to book you?"

"I'm already taking reservations for next Christmas," Holiday said. "I get a ton of repeat customers."

"And how—" Janine cut herself off. "Sorry, I was trained as a research librarian. I have a lot of questions."

"We have nothing but time and the open road." Holiday gestured toward the vast expanse of snow and sky outside the Jeep. "Ask away."

"How long have you been doing this full-time?"

"Five years, at least." Holiday paused. "Ever since I decided not to get married."

"What? Talk about burying the lede! Tell me every—" Janine's question gave way to a panicked scream as a moose galloped out from the tree line and in front of the car. She slammed on the brakes and Holiday joined in on the second round of screaming as the car screeched to a stop inches away from the animal's retreating flanks.

Just as the women breathed a sigh of relief, a second moose darted in front of the car, moving so quickly that one of its rear hooves clipped the Jeep's bumper as it passed. Holiday instinctively threw one hand against the dashboard and the other over her face. After a few thundering heartbeats, she resumed breathing and lowered her arms.

Janine was braced with both hands on the wheel, her face ashen and her eyes wide. After a moment, she drew a shuddering breath. "Whew. That was a close one."

"Was that . . ." Holiday had to stop and swallow. "A

moose?"

"Two," Janine confirmed. "Which is odd, because they usually travel alone." She released her death grip on the steering wheel. "But it's okay. We're okay." She turned to Holiday. "You're okay, right?"

Holiday found herself unable to speak. But she was definitely not okay. Her hands reached for the door handle and the seat belt release, and her body heaved itself out of the car and onto the windswept highway.

Janine leaned across the passenger seat. "Holiday? What are you doing?"

Holiday turned away from the car to face the snow and the pine trees. "I can't do this. I thought I could, but I can't."

"You can't do what?" Janine called.

Holiday took a few steps so that she was off the asphalt and in the shallow snow drifts. "I can't do any of this. I can't drive in this weather, I can't almost hit a moose, I can't hunt down the random ancestors of an artist for DNA, and I can't make Alex fall in love with Mrs. Penewate's granddaughter. I can't do any of it."

The car's engine rumbled to a halt and the driver's-side door slammed as Janine got out of the car.

"I can't." Holiday crossed her arms to ward off the frigid wind. "I can't give everyone what they want and still be home for Christmas. I should never have agreed to this job."

Janine joined her at the side of the road. "So, quit."

Holiday shook her head and took another step into the snowdrift. "I can't quit, either."

"Sure, you can. It's easy. Just call the lady who hired you, explain the situation, and refund her money. No big deal."

"Very big deal." Holiday bowed her head. "I already failed her once." Standing in the snow like this released a barrage of memories, both personal and professional. She tried to keep her focus on the professional. "Alice Penewate's husband hired me two years ago. I let him down, and I'll never make up for it."

"Tell me what happened." Janine's voice was soothing, and her hand tugged Holiday's elbow. "When you're not knee-deep in snow."

Holiday looked down and realized that ice crystals were indeed melting into her jeans. "Alice and her husband, James, got married on Christmas Eve on the spur of the moment in Atlantic City. This was like sixty years ago."

"Come on, your pants are getting soaked," Janine coaxed.

"And they went to some bar to celebrate, and at the end of the night, the bar owner gave them the record the bartender had been playing over and over on the jukebox." She could remember every detail of the target item. "The Five Keys' 'It's Christmas Time' from Aladdin Records, with a blue label."

"Okay, sounds good. Let's get back in the car."

But Holiday remained where she stood, welcoming the tiny bursts of cold as snowflakes fell onto her face. "I went online, found some vinyl collecting chat boards, and tracked down a copy of the record with a private collector near Reno. He was a crotchety old coot, stuck in the previous century, and he absolutely refused to sell me the record over the phone." She bristled at the memory. "Said he had other interested buyers and whoever showed up in person first would get it. He was the worst."

Janine gave up on getting back to the car and settled into the snowbank with her. The forest around them was completely silent.

"Someone beat you to it?" Janine asked.

"Heck, no," Holiday scoffed. "I was on the first flight to Nevada. I played his game, showed up at the store, and paid his overinflated asking price in cash." She paused. "The problem was, it was snowing. Just like today."

"Please don't tell me you hit a moose in Nevada."

"I didn't hit anything. But I also didn't have four-wheel drive in my rental car and I didn't have much experience driving in the snow."

"So I gathered," Janine said.

Holiday ignored this. "The snow got worse and worse, and pretty soon, I was sliding all over the road and I couldn't see anything. I had to turn on my hazard lights and pull over. And I was only planning to be in Reno for a few hours, so all I had was my purse, a little carry-on, and that record. I kept thinking, it could be hours before someone digs me out of here. I figured I was going to have to walk to the nearest gas station or whatever, so I gathered up my stuff, got out of the car, and started walking."

"This story is a downer," Janine said.

"Oh, it gets worse. Almost as soon as I get out of the car, I see headlights, and it's a snowplow. So I figure I can start up the car and follow the plow back into town and still make my flight. I got all excited and turned around really fast—and fell right on my face." She closed her eyes at the memory. "And everything I was holding went flying."

"But the record was in the sleeve inside your little bag?" Janine clarified.

"It was." Holiday nodded. "But that still couldn't protect it from cracking when the snowplow ran it over."

Janine winced. "Oh no."

"Oh yes." Holiday tightened her crossed arms. "It was awful. I had assured Mr. Penewate that I could get this record, no sweat, and I had it in my hands. I *had* it."

"But it was an accident. You tripped."

"And somebody's fondest wish shattered into a dozen pieces. And that was it. I was out of time and that record is almost impossible to get. I had to call James and tell him I failed. I had to quit."

"There were a lot of extenuating circumstances," Janine said. "And the good thing about Christmas is that it comes around every twelve months. Couldn't you just have a do-over the next year?"

"No. James Penewate died two weeks after I was supposed to deliver the record to him."

"Oh boy."

"And now I have a phobia of failure, a phobia of snow, and a phobia of driving in the snow. Plus a brand-new phobia of moose."

Janine smiled wryly and opened her arms. "Welcome to Maine."

"I can't do this." She sighed in resignation.

"You can and you will. You have a seasoned chauffeur, a Jeep, and a mission. Don't let a few rogue moose rattle you."

"Too late."

"Move along." Janine prodded her back toward the car and, this time, Holiday went. "You're going to redeem yourself with Mrs. Penewate. And in the meantime, you're going to tell me why you decided not to get married five years ago and what that has to do with being a Christmas concierge."

"I can't." Holiday shook her head. "I'm already having a nervous breakdown."

"Fine. Have it in the car." Janine herded her into the passenger seat. "Watch your head."

"You Mainers are mean," Holiday told her.

"Yeah, but we get stuff done." Janine jogged around to the driver's side, buckled her seat belt, and started the engine. "Now. Did you remember to bring the vial and the Q-tip?"

Holiday opened her bag and pulled out the DIY genetics kit. "Check and check. Now all I have to do is figure out the best way to convince a total stranger to cough up their DNA."

Chapter Nine

"NO." PAMELA DONOVAN wouldn't even let Holiday over the threshold to her home. "Heck, no."

"I know this sounds a little wacky." Holiday kept her voice low and light. "But if you'll give me a moment to explain . . ."

"Save your breath." The woman crossed her arms and narrowed her eyes. "I'm not falling for this."

"But you don't even know what 'this' is."

"Here's what I know." Pamela, clad in baggy jeans and an oversized red flannel shirt, scowled. "I know that if someone shows up at my house unannounced and asks to rub a Q-tip in my cheek, I should say no."

"I can't argue with that logic." Holiday took a step back on the porch to give the other woman some space. "But this actually is more about your great-granduncle, Driscoll Davidson."

"Really." Pamela sidled forward, her expression cagey. "Why didn't you say that in the first place?"

Holiday decided that this was not the time to point out that Pamela had been shouting her down with "No!" every time she opened her mouth. "We're trying to track down some of his relatives . . ."

"What did you say your name was again?"

Holiday, who had already given Pamela her business card, offered her a second one. "Holiday Smith. I'm what's known as a Christmas concierge."

Pamela didn't even glance at the card. "Did my second cousin Bob send you?"

"What? No."

"Because I've told him a hundred times, I'm never speaking to him again." Pamela seized the snow shovel propped against the doorjamb and banged it against the porch floor for emphasis.

"I'm on an independent mission," Holiday swore. "I don't know any details about the Davidson family rift, and I don't need to know."

"Then how did you get my name and address?"

Holiday explained the truncated family tree situation as quickly as possible. "So if you can help me find any other relatives who might have some of Driscoll's original pieces, I'd be forever grateful."

"I can't," Pamela stated flatly. "No one talks to those traitors."

"Well, then, the next best thing would be some DNA, so I can try to track them down through a database."

Pamela shook the shovel again. "Are you *sure* Bob didn't send you?"

"Scout's honor." Holiday raised her palm. "Please. This has nothing to do with your family issues, I swear." She summarized the situation with Alex and Paul's mother as succinctly as possible. "Help a bereaved widow's Christmas wish come true."

Pamela's expression softened. Her grip on the snow shovel loosened. Then she snapped back into her scowl. "I'm no sucker." She started to close the door.

"Wait!" Holiday opened the flap on her purse. "I'll pay you!"

"That's just what my second cousin Bob would say. Merry Christmas." *Slam.*

Holiday trudged through the fresh powder with her head hung low. As soon as she opened the passenger door to the Jeep, Janine peppered her with questions.

"What happened? I couldn't see anybody's faces." And then she saw Holiday's expression. "Uh-oh. No joy?"

"Ugh." Holiday flopped against the seatback and peeled off her gloves. "She thought I was some sort of mole sent by her second cousin Bob."

"Okay, well, who else is on the list?" Janine bounced in her seat, undeterred. "Scratch off Pamela Donovan. The next closest known relative lives in . . ." They peered down at Holiday's list of possible DNA sources. "Ohio."

"No, no, no, no." Holiday took a deep breath. "That's not feasible. Let's regroup for a second. All the private investigators I know are out of the office until January. So. Let me pull up the trash collection schedule for this part of town." She swiped through her phone.

"Because . . .?"

"Once someone puts their trash bin out by the curb, it's considered public property," Holiday explained. "So we might get lucky and be able to salvage a thrown-out tissue, a toothbrush, whatever."

Janine grimaced. "'We'?"

"That's right. You wanted to go on this quest with me, you have to go all the way into the dumpster."

"Tough but fair." Janine nodded and accepted her fate.

They both jumped as a sharp tap on the window interrupted Holiday's trash reconnaissance. A tall, lanky teenager in a gray beanie was trying to get their attention.

Holiday glanced at Janine and rolled the window down two inches. "Hello?"

"Hey, did you guys say you needed some spit?" The youth was at least six foot four, wearing only denim overalls and a threadbare tie-dyed T-shirt. He seemed impervious to the cold.

"Who are you?" Holiday demanded.

"I'm her son." The kid jerked his thumb toward the farmhouse up on the hill. "I heard you and my mom talking. Listen, if you need Davidson DNA, I'll give you some."

Holiday smiled. "That's sweet of you. I really appreciate it, but you're not old enough to give away your DNA without your parents' permission. They could file a lawsuit, we'll all have to hire attorneys, and it'll be a whole thing."

He looked offended. "I'm nineteen."

Holiday squinted at the scruffy facial hair and bushy eyebrows partially obscuring his plump, pink baby face. "You are not."

"Am too!"

"Let's see some ID," Janine demanded.

He dug around his overall pockets until he located a

driver's license. "Read it and weep."

Holiday studied the photo, name, and birthdate on the Maine driver's license. She held it up and turned it over in the sunlight like a bouncer about to bust a marauding high schooler. "Is this real?"

"Yes!" He threw up his hands. "Who walks around with a fake ID at their own house in the middle of the morning?"

A decent point. "And you're a direct, biological descendant of Driscoll Davidson?" she pressed.

"Yeah, but we're not supposed to talk about it because my mom gets mad."

Holiday looked at Janine. Janine looked back.

"What do you have to lose?" Janine asked.

"You better hurry up," the kid said. "If my mom sees me talking to you, it's all over."

Holiday quick ran a risk-benefit analysis and decided that taking her chances on a legal adult with valid ID was a better bet than risking her future on the vagaries of trash collection.

"Okay, how much do you want?" she asked him.

He mulled this over for a moment. "A new laptop."

"Fine. Scrape this on the inside of your cheek for fifteen seconds and send me a link for the computer you want." She handed him the at-home DNA collection materials. "Is your mom's address okay for shipping the laptop?"

"Works for me." As he unscrewed the vial's cap and extracted the swab, a woman's voice bellowed down the hill from the house.

"Jonah, what you doing? Jonah, get away from that car!"

But it was too late. Fifteen seconds had passed, the cheek cells were collected, and the vial was back in Holiday's hands.

"Thanks, kid." She pressed her business card into his palm. "My direct email is printed right there. Don't forget to send me that link. Tell you what, I'll throw in some top-of-the-line headphones for your troubles."

"Wow, thanks, lady!"

Pamela Donovan emerged from the house, wielding the snow shovel like an axe. "Get off my property right now or I'm calling the cops!"

Holiday turned to Janine. "Punch it."

Janine punched it. The Jeep fishtailed down the long gravel driveway, spraying snow and gravel in its wake.

"This is great!" Janine laughed. "It's like the rebellious adolescence I never had." She rolled down the window and *woo-hooed* into the wind.

Before Holiday could join in, her cell phone buzzed in her coat pocket. "Hang on," she told Janine, who rolled the window back up.

Holiday pressed the phone close to her ear. "Mom?"

"Hi, hon."

"How's it going?"

"Fine. Why are you yelling?" her mother asked.

"Sorry." Holiday tried to take it down a notch. "Just the chills and thrills that go with my job."

"I'm so glad to finally get ahold of you. I keep calling and it just goes straight to voice mail."

"That's because the hotel where I'm staying is stuck in

1985, technology-wise," Holiday said.

"Good lord. Where on earth are you?"

"Maine."

"I thought you were going to be in the Midwest some-where," her mother said. "Iowa? Idaho?"

"That was last week."

"I can't keep track of all your comings and goings." There was a loud, metallic banging on Mom's end of the line.

"What are you doing?" Holiday asked.

"Baking." Her mother's voice sounded strained. "Just getting this mixer out from under the cabinet counts as strength training."

"Ooh, what are you making? Are you making the coco-nut macaroons?"

"Of course! And gingerbread, sugar cookies, and the spritz cookies from your grandmother's recipe."

"Save some of the spritz cookies for me," Holiday begged.

"Yes, as to that . . ." More clinking and clanging from her mother's end. "Nora said you might actually make it home for Christmas this time."

Holiday paused, glancing at the DNA sample on the dashboard. "Well. That is my hope."

"To hear Nora tell it, you swore up and down and left and right that you'd be here."

"I mean . . . yes, that is what I said—"

"Great! I'm so excited, Holl! It's been too long since we all had Christmas morning as a family. I'll make up the bed in the guest room with those flannel sheets you like, I'll hang up your stocking, and I'll make some extra cinnamon rolls."

Holiday closed her eyes, picturing the scene. "That all sounds amazing."

"Keep me posted on when you'll be here and if we can do anything to help, okay?"

"Will do." Holiday's eyes closed tighter as guilt and doubt crept in. "But Mom?"

"Yes, dear?" This time Holiday recognized the sound on the other end of the line—metal measuring spoons rattling against a glass measuring cup.

"Nothing. Tell Dad I say hi, okay? Love you." Holiday ended the call and opened her eyes to the harsh sunlight glinting off sheets of ice.

"Family drama?" Janine asked.

"*I'm* the drama. The rest of the family is great." She did some mental calculations. "But depending on how fast Alex can get the DNA results back, I might still be able to get home by Christmas."

"What I hear you saying is, you need a miracle and/or a fast driver." Janine cranked up the radio. "It's your lucky day, lady."

Chapter Ten

"*VOILA*." HOLIDAY STRODE into the seaplane charter building and into the back office, which was clearly marked NO ADMITTANCE. "I have returned triumphant."

Alex glanced away from his computer screen, which was crowded with spreadsheets. "You got the tree topper?"

"No, but I got us one step closer." She placed the DNA kit on the desk and slid it toward him.

He glanced at it with dawning admiration. "Is that what I think it is?"

"If you think it's a buccal swab from one of Driscoll Davidson's long-lost relatives, then you are correct."

He nodded. "Get it off my desk, please."

She slid the box back into the padded envelope. "And PS, it cost me a top-of-the line laptop and professional-quality gaming headphones. I'll put it on your tab." She glanced around the office. "So where's Paul?"

"He is taking a group of winter campers to an island up north."

"Winter camping?" She shivered at the very idea. "Sounds horrible. When will he be back? The clock is ticking and this DNA sample's losing freshness by the minute."

"That's not really how it works." Alex resumed typing

numbers into his spreadsheet.

"Hey!" She smacked her palm down on the desktop. "This is a code-red, nine-one-one, all-hands-on-deck situation here. I need a genetic profile, *stat*."

He didn't even glance away from the monitor. "A few hours doesn't really make any difference."

"It does to me! I'm trying to get home for Christmas." She provided the bullet points on her promise to her sister. "And now my mother is putting the red flannel sheets on my bed and prepping cinnamon rolls! I have to be there. Failure is not an option."

"Okay, okay." He leaned back in his chair. "You'll be there." Before she could protest further, he pulled out his cell phone. "Let me make some calls. The DNA sample will be delivered, analyzed, and returned by tomorrow at eight a.m."

"Are you sure?"

"You keep your hastily made promises, I'll keep mine." He smiled. "And please never divulge the details of how you got this DNA, so I can maintain plausible deniability."

"No worries."

He gazed back up at her. "You want some coffee?"

She glanced at the huge, stainless steel espresso machine on the counter. "No thanks. I'm fine."

"No, I mean, would you like to go *get* some coffee? While we're waiting for Paul?"

Holiday blinked. Was he asking her out? "Like, just coffee? Just as friends? Friends who like coffee?"

Alex's face looked as though he might actually be blushing underneath the stubble. "Yeah. That."

The phone on his desk rang, startling both of them. Alex glanced at caller ID. "I've got to get this."

"Of course." She cleared her throat and slid the padded envelope toward him. "I'll just leave this here." She backed out of the office and closed the door behind her. She could hear his voice for a moment or two, and then silence. She wasn't sure if she should stay or go. Was the friendly coffee get-together on or off?

She raised her hand to knock, then let it drop. If she was honest with herself, she had to admit that nothing good could come out of spending more time with Alex. He wasn't hers to spend time with. He was Alice Penewate's Christmas bounty, and Holiday intended to deliver him as promised. Her life, including her heart—*especially* her heart—was on hold until January second.

HOLIDAY AWOKE AT dawn the next morning and rolled out of bed, preparing to bundle up and head out into the frigid sunrise in search of cell service. But before she could even take off her pajamas, she noticed an envelope had been slipped under the hotel room door. It was impossible to miss the white paper rectangle in such stark contrast to the mint-and-pink carpet, even in dim lighting.

She pounced on the envelope, which bore her name in neat capital letters. The message inside was jotted on a yellow piece of legal paper:

DNA results came back. See attached. Hope this helps

and let me know if you need anything else. A.

She ignored the fluttering in her stomach and focused her energies on turning on the lamp and studying the packet of genealogy information, of which she could decipher about forty percent. She definitely needed some help, but not from Alex.

One hour later, Holiday settled at a rustic wooden table drenched in sunlight by the front window of the Wily Whale. Janine was waiting, clad in baggy pajamas and shearling boots, already halfway through a cup of coffee.

"What took you so long?" She slid a second, full mug of coffee across the table to Holiday.

"I got here as fast as I could." Holiday unwound her knitted scarf.

"You took the time to get dressed," Janine observed. "That's what slowed you down."

"Misplaced priorities," Holiday conceded.

"All right, I'm ready to play detective." Janine fired up her laptop and held out her hand for the envelope. "Gimme."

Holiday passed over the paperwork. "Do they have any pastries here? I feel like butter and carbs help me do my best work."

"The bear claws are to die for." Janine started typing in codes and creating login profiles. "Get two."

Holiday signaled to the server at the counter, then peered at the laptop screen. "So what are we doing, exactly?"

"Well, we have some genealogy information from the family tree." Janine brought up the picture of the document she'd stored on her phone. "These DNA results might help fill in the blanks if another relative has also submitted their DNA for profiling. Keep your fingers crossed that someone in the missing branches has an interest in ancestry and/or is just plain nosy."

Holiday crossed fingers on both of her hands.

"Okay . . ." Janine typed furiously. "Okay . . ."

"The suspense is killing me."

"Don't worry. The bear claws will bring you back to life." Janine's brow furrowed as she frowned at the computer. "Huh."

Holiday nearly strained a muscle as she craned her neck to get a better view. "What do you mean, 'huh'? 'Huh' doesn't sound very promising."

"Simmer down. I just have to add some information." Janine patted her hand. "Maybe you should downgrade to decaf."

After several minutes of typing and pastry consumption, Janine pushed her chair back a few inches. "Well, well, well. Look who has a great-grandson living in New Hampshire."

"And he's from the x-ed-out side of the tree? The side that's supposed to have all the good stuff they took out of spite?"

Janine consulted the original genealogy tree. "He must be, because I don't see him or his parents' names on here anywhere."

"And you're sure that he's a direct descent of Driscoll?" Holiday pressed.

"I'm sure that this DNA website *says* he is." Janine treated herself to a big bite of bear claw to reward herself for expert-level internet sleuthery. "But you're going to have to take it from here."

"With pleasure." Holiday laced her palms together and flexed her fingers as she prepared to take over the keyboard. "May I?"

"Please do."

In the space of five minutes, Holiday had run the name Janine produced through multiple court systems, property records, and a private-pay background checker.

"Behold, Crispin Kilgorff the Third." Holiday gestured to the screen with a flourish. "Clean driving record, no felonies or misdemeanors, and owner of a five-acre estate near Lake Sheridan, New Hampshire."

"Ooh, fancy." Janine crooked her little finger as she took a sip of coffee.

"Is it?"

Janine looked wistful. "I'd live there for sure, if I had a boatload of family money."

"And leave all this?" Holiday held out one arm to encompass the ocean, the pine trees, and the pastry.

"This could be my second home," Janine allowed. "Or third."

"How long is the drive to Lake Sheridan?" Holiday pulled up some map sites. "About three hours?"

"I mean, if the weather holds off." Janine glanced up at the clear morning sky. "Rumor has it that there's a blizzard on the way."

Holiday's chest tightened. "You know my history with

blizzards."

"Yeah, but don't worry—it's not supposed to really start snowing until Christmas Eve."

"Christmas Eve is tomorrow," Holiday pointed out.

Janine's eyes widened. "It is? It is not. It can't be."

"You just told me the weather and the genetic history of Crispin Kilgorff the Third. How can you not know what day it is?"

"I can't be an expert on everything. I'm only one woman." Janine shot to her feet and gathered up her coat and laptop. "I've got to go shopping immediately."

"If you want to give everyone on your list a deeply discounted subscription for DNA kits, I can hook you up," Holiday offered.

"If you ever met my mother, you would know how hilarious that is." Janine pulled out her car keys. "She only likes fussy, antique decorative crap that I'm terrible at picking out."

"Then there's no need to go shopping," Holiday said. "Just come loot my hotel room, aka Laura Ashley's last stand."

"She loves Laura Ashley." Janine pointed to her pajamas, which featured pants festooned with cartoon rainbow-striped unicorns and a threadbare shirt emblazoned with "QUESTION AUTHORITY." "We're pretty sure there was a mix-up at the hospital. Anyway, I better run."

"Good luck," Holiday called as Janine headed for the door. "Call me if you need suggestions. I'm really good at this."

"And spoil the suspense? It's not really Christmas until you've had a migraine and a crying jag," Janine called back.

And then she was gone, leaving Holiday alone with the name and number of the man who might hold the key to pulling off a Christmas hat trick—Alex Sappier's tree topper, Francie Penewate's dream date, and Holiday's homecoming. She glanced at her watch. She had about thirty-six hours to pull this off. Three hours each way to New Hampshire, plus a few hours to arrange the most romantic date in the world, plus meals and trips to the restroom . . . should be fine. *Fine.* Everything was *just fine.*

If the blizzard held off.

And Crispin Kilgorff the Third didn't turn out to be a dead end.

And Francie Penewate didn't have any travel complications on the way to Alemos Island.

That was a lot of *ifs*. Holiday assured herself that she had been on much tighter deadlines before. She had overcome much greater odds to emerge unscathed and victorious.

She just couldn't remember when, exactly.

But she didn't have time for self-doubt or second thoughts right now. Right now, she had to keep pushing forward, rely on her considerable powers of persuasion, and hope for a little luck.

She took a deep, coffee-scented breath and dialed her cell phone. "Hello, I'm calling for a Mr. Crispin Kilgorff, please?"

Chapter Eleven

THIRTY MINUTES LATER, Holiday was on the road and headed for the bridge to the mainland with a thermal mug of lukewarm coffee in her cupholder and a paper bag full of healthful snacks in the back seat. Mr. Kilgorff had responded to her inquiries in the exact opposite manner than his long-lost fourth cousin (or whatever) Pamela.

"Yes, I'm well aware of my great-grandfather's penchant for dramatics," Crispin had informed her. "My mother liked to say he had an 'artistic temperament.' There are still boxes of old heirlooms up in the attic, but no one's been up there in years. You're welcome to come and go through them, if you like."

Twinges of suspicion stirred in her gut. This seemed a bit too easy . . . but wasn't she due for a little luck? She should stop being so pessimistic and count her blessings.

The moment she allowed herself to revel in her good fortune, the steering wheel jerked in her hands and the little sedan started sliding on a patch of black ice. She yanked at the wheel and stomped on the brake, to no avail. For a few weightless, breathless moments, she saw the world whirl around her until—*thunk*—one tire skidded off the icy asphalt and into a snowbank.

Holiday sat back to relieve the pressure of the safety belt restraining her chest. She closed her eyes and concentrated on regulating her breathing, despite the adrenaline flooding through her body. She felt simultaneously grateful that she hadn't been injured and irate that the rental car company had given away her all-wheel-drive vehicle to someone else.

She glanced toward the bridge, imagining how icy the pavement must be over the gray churning water, since—as the sign plainly stated—BRIDGE FREEZES BEFORE ROAD. She checked the weather on her phone, hoping against hope that the forecast would change, but no—the app insisted that the temperature would hover in the low thirties all day before plummeting at sundown.

She needed to get to Lake Sheridan ASAP, but she also needed to stay alive in order to complete her missions. There had to be a better way to work this out. And with that, a pickup truck crested over the horizon. A heavy-duty pickup truck with studded snow tires and a familiar driver behind the wheel.

Holiday scrambled out of the sedan and jumped up and down, waving her hands. The pickup slowed, and Alex rolled down the window.

He glanced at her, then her car, then the snowbank. "You stuck?"

"Kind of. Where are you going?" she asked.

"Home. I just had to pick up a few things from the mainland."

"I'm so glad to hear that. I need to borrow your truck."

Alex started shaking his head, but she interjected before

he could protest. "Look at my car. And look at this road. There's no way I'm going to make it to New Hampshire and back without incurring major damage and possibly death."

"What's in New Hampshire?" he asked.

"Your Christmas miracle, hopefully. Trade keys with me," she demanded.

"No."

"Do you want your tree topper or not?" She put her hands on her hips.

He hesitated, and she thought she had him. Then he resumed shaking his head. "The truck stays with me."

"Oh, come on. What do you think I'm going to do to it?"

He paused again, considering. "Nothing. I just don't like—"

"'Being strong-armed into other people's agendas'?" She arched one eyebrow as she quoted his own words back at him.

His smile looked a bit sheepish. "You remembered."

"Fine, then get ready for a road trip to scenic New Hampshire." She held out her palm. "At least give me the keys. I'll drive."

He glanced pointedly at the car in the snowbank.

"That wasn't my fault. Blame it on the stupid car. The road conditions are ridiculous." She started hopping up and down. "Let's go, time's a-wastin'."

Alex opened the truck door and climbed out. "Listen, if we drive all the way to New Hampshire—and I am not making any promises as to who will be driving—you can't leave your car here. It's supposed to snow this afternoon, which means they'll plow the roads again. Best-case scenario, your car will get buried. Worst-case scenario, it's going to get smashed up six ways from Sunday."

"The curse of the snowplow strikes again." Holiday shuddered.

He blinked. "What?"

"Nothing." She set her jaw. "I knew I should have sprung for the extra insurance coverage."

"Drive to that parking lot." He pointed out the drugstore across the street. "Leave it there, unlocked, and put the keys in the glove compartment. I'll have Paul come over later and move it to the hotel."

"Leave it unlocked?" Holiday was scandalized.

"Don't worry." He started back toward his truck. "It's Alemos Island."

She stared at him, sizing him up. "And you're not going to take off and leave me truckless?"

"I want that tree topper," he said. "We're a team now."

"Yes, we are." She sighed inwardly. "Until tomorrow night."

"Then we better hit the road, teammate."

"ALEX, THIS IS nice of you, but you really don't have to go with me all the way to Lake Sheridan and back." Holiday rested her hands at ten and two o'clock on the steering wheel. After a spirited negotiation, they had decided to take turns driving.

"I can't take any chances," he replied. "I need that tree topper and time is running out. My mom keeps asking questions and I can't put her off forever."

She glanced at the digital clock on the dashboard. "Since we have hours to kill, why don't you tell me about this tree topper and why you're willing to romance a stranger for it?"

"The short version is, I screwed up, and when I screw up, I fix it."

"We still have four more hours, minimum. Go ahead and tell me the long version."

He took off his jacket and settled in for the ride. "My parents were married for almost forty years. My dad was a pilot in the Air Force, which meant we moved a lot. It was a great opportunity for a kid—I got to live in Alaska, Arizona, Germany, Japan, South Korea, and a bunch of other places—but since we were constantly packing up to relocate, we kind of thinned our possessions down to the bare minimum."

"So that tree topper got some serious mileage," Holiday said.

"Like Paul said before, it was a wedding gift from some rich relative. My parents did okay financially, but they never could have swung a fancy collector's piece like that. My mom was crazy about it. Every Christmas she'd unwrap it from twenty layers of Bubble Wrap and tissue paper and tell us the story of the first Christmas she had with my dad. Every time we moved, she made sure that she personally packaged that star because she didn't trust the movers to do it. That star went around the globe with us until my dad retired from the service."

"Where did they end up living?" Holiday asked.

"They were in the Boston suburbs for a long time. Paul and I both went to college in Massachusetts."

"So I learned during my extensive background investigation," Holiday assured him.

Alex rolled his eyes. "If you did such a meticulous background check on me, shouldn't you already know who my parents were and where they lived?"

"You're the target, not your parents," she said. "I have boundaries."

"You commandeered my truck in broad daylight," he pointed out.

"And I graciously permitted you to go with me on my mission," Holiday said. "Since your name is on the vehicle registration and all. Like I said, boundaries."

"Anyway, my parents lived near Boston while my brother and I went to college, and my mom went back to school and got her master's in social work. She was working with an eldercare agency, and my dad was helping Paul start the charter plane business."

"While you were giving commencement addresses and taking the tech world by storm," Holiday finished for him. "And flying hither and yon in your company's private jet."

"It sounds more exciting than it really was. I had a lot of research interests and a lot of money, but no time." He looked exhausted just thinking about it. "I practically lived at work—I had a fold-down couch in my office so I could sleep there—and I had a fancy condo in Back Bay that I barely saw."

"But you didn't care because it was a good investment," she predicted.

"Yes." He shot her a glance. "Did I already tell you this part?"

"No, but the vast majority of my clients have way more money than free time. I know the drill."

"There came a tipping point when I realized I had more than enough money, but my time was finite. So I invested accordingly and moved up here."

Holiday studied his expression, which appeared totally neutral. "What was the tipping point?"

"Eyes on the road." He pointed at the windshield.

"Was it a moral dilemma? A health crisis?" She paused, then pushed ahead with the question she was most curious about. "A bad breakup?"

"We're talking about my mom," he reminded her.

"We're going to be spending the whole day together," she repeated. "Might as well tell me all your deep, dark secrets."

"That's not necessary," he assured her. "How about a podcast instead?"

He reached for the radio dial. She swatted his hand away. "Maybe later. Right now, I'd like to hear the incredible true story of how a guy like you ends up single in the middle of nowhere."

He pretended to take offense. "First of all, I like living in the middle of nowhere."

"Fair enough." Holiday circled her hand to prompt him to continue. "And you're single because . . ."

He rolled his eyes. "I already told you. I'm a soulless sociopath."

She burst out laughing. "Give it up, Sappier. No one's buying that. I already heard about you personally rebuilding the elementary school."

He muttered darkly about Sally under his breath.

"And besides, sociopaths don't send you grilled cheese and tomato soup, so you won't go to bed hungry." She pointed at her eyes, then at his. "I see you, Alex. *I see you.*"

He finally shrugged and relented. "Okay, fine, you got me. I had a bad breakup."

"Just as I suspected." She took a sip of coffee and prepared to hear his tale.

"But it turned out to be the best thing that ever happened to me, so it really wasn't that bad," he continued.

"Very philosophical of you." Holiday adjusted the windshield wiper setting.

"I was dating a woman named Kathryn—"

"Model?" Holiday guessed. "Actress?"

"CEO," he corrected. "She was also in biotech. My problem is, I like women who are smart and successful."

Her eyebrows shot all the way up. "I can't wait to hear why that's a problem."

He paused for a moment, choosing his words carefully. "When you have two people who are both used to running the show and being in charge . . . conflicts can arise."

She put the coffee down. "Such as . . .?"

He remained carefully neutral and even-toned. "I ran my life my way, she ran her life her way, but when we started to get serious . . ." He trailed off, rubbing his chin. "I think the problems started when she started messing with my phone."

Holiday waited for him to elaborate.

"First, she didn't like my ringtone, and that was no big deal, so I let her go ahead and change it. But then she wanted to change the way I organized my calendar."

Holiday frowned. "Like, your online calendar?"

"Yeah. We had a ridiculous fight about that." He sucked in his breath at the memory. "And then my administrative assistant got involved. She got madder than anybody else because she was actually in charge of my schedule."

"Yeah, don't mess with the person who organizes your office life."

"It's a miracle I'm still alive." He shuddered. "Kathryn and I took a few vacations together and had a great time, but when she came to my condo, she started changing the kitchen without talking to me."

"Changing it how?" Holiday barely had the time, energy, and motivation to organize her own living space, let alone anyone else's.

"Rearranging the cabinets and the pantry. I know it sounds like no big deal—"

"Not really."

"But after she left, I couldn't find my coffee or my coffee cup, and I was late to work for the first time in my life."

"Hold on." Holiday put up her palm and called for a time-out. "I need to make sure I'm understanding this. So she just . . . moved all your dishes?"

"And the silverware, the pots, and the appliances." He nodded. "She said her way was more efficient."

"But she didn't live with you, correct?"

"Correct. She just came over on weekends."

This was all Holiday needed to deliver her verdict. "She sounds like a micromanaging control freak."

He smiled but didn't join her in disparaging Kathryn. "I'm only telling my side of the story," he said. "I'm sure when she tells it, it's very different. In her version, I'm probably stubborn and short on counter space. With bad taste in ringtones."

"Now I have to know what your ringtone was."

He very pointedly ignored that. "A few weeks after the kitchen overhaul, she started looking at engagement rings without me and texting me pictures of the ones she liked."

"And that's the end of that story?" Holiday guessed.

"Pretty much. We had one last fight—right around this time of year, actually. Then she got recruited by a start-up in Silicon Valley and moved to California. I wanted to get away from the traffic and the crowds, so I moved up here."

"So your heart would freeze and you'd never fall in love again?" she teased.

"So I could think about how I really wanted to spend my life," he corrected.

She softened her tone. "Was it hard when she left?"

He thought about this. "Yeah. But a lot of that was about who I saw myself becoming. Impatient. Short-tempered. Narrow-minded."

Holiday blinked. "You don't seem like any of those things to me."

"I was having two-hour arguments about silverware drawers." He sounded deeply chagrined. "That's not who I want to be. There are real, urgent problems in this world, and the location of my toaster is not one of them." He glanced at her. "You know how sometimes, when someone is driving you crazy, and you take a second to look at your life, you realize that the thing that irritates you about them is the thing that really irritates you about yourself?"

She nodded. "I am sorry to say that yes, I am familiar with that feeling."

"Kathryn was a . . . what did you call it? A micromanager?" He laughed ruefully. "And so was I. We micromanaged ourselves, we micromanaged our employees, we tried to micromanage each other. And you know what I discovered? Micromanaging sucks. It's also exhausting."

"This explains why you're so madcap and reckless now," she deadpanned.

"I have great people doing great work who don't need me breathing down their necks every day. They need funding and freedom to do their jobs, so that's what I give them." He shrugged one shoulder. "And myself. They know they can always reach out if they need me."

"So life out here is good for your soul," she concluded. "I get it. It's starting to win me over, too—all the fresh air and the open space and the ocean views . . ."

"It's not perfect, but I'll take bridge closures and bad coffee over rush hour on the expressway any day."

Holiday gasped. "Bad coffee? How dare you malign the Wily Whale."

"The Wily Whale is a great place to go for pizza and beer," he allowed. "They do the best with what they have, but it's no match for the cafés in the city that roast their beans daily."

"You're a coffee snob." She nodded as she absorbed this. "Would not have predicted that."

"Add it to my long list of flaws. Anyway, my parents were going to move up here, too, and do a whole second-career thing, but then my dad died suddenly last year. Heart attack."

"I'm so sorry."

"A month or two after he passed, my mom decided to sell the house and downsize. She found an agency up here that needed social workers, so she agreed to let me rent her a two-bedroom house on the island until she was ready to make more permanent decisions."

"You're renting a house for your mom?" Holiday gushed. "That is so sweet."

"Actually, I bought it," he confessed. "But she doesn't know that."

"Let me guess—good investment?"

"The real estate market is getting insane up here. She's doing her best, but it's her first Christmas without my dad and she said she wasn't in the mood to decorate. So Paul and I offered to put up all the decorations for her." He paused. "And here we are."

"What have you told her by way of explanation?"

He cleared his throat. "The official story is that it's somewhere in my garage, and I haven't had time to search for it yet."

"It's December twenty-third," Holiday pointed out.

"Yes, well, that's why that excuse is wearing thin. She's threatening to come over and go through my garage herself."

"Which would be bad."

"So bad." He blew out a breath and shook his head.

"And if you just come clean and tell her that you broke it—"

"Technically, Paul broke it," he interjected.

"That's not what Paul said," she reminded him.

"I'm your client and I'm saying Paul broke it."

She laughed. "Fair enough. If you come clean and tell her that Paul broke it . . ."

"*So* bad."

"Have no fear. We are going to look on the bright side," Holiday declared. "Crispin Kilgorff the Third assured me that there are boxes of mystery treasures in his attic, and I am going to think positive thoughts that there is a forty-year-old tree topper that is a dead ringer for the one that you—excuse me, that *Paul*—broke."

"Positive thoughts? That's where we are with this? We might as well break out the crystals and incantations." Alex groaned in despair. "And we're staking my mom's Christmas on some guy named Crispin Kilgorff the Third?"

"He sounded very nice on the phone." Holiday took another sip from her thermal mug. "I take it that you don't want any of my subpar coffee?"

"I don't want your coffee," he confirmed. "I want *your* deep, dark secrets."

She tried to look bemused. "You're going to have to be more specific."

"I told you mine, you tell me yours. It's only fair."

"Well, let's see." She feigned great concentration. "I can tell you right now that my ringtone is 'Reflection' and my text tone is 'Chime.'"

He wasn't about to let her off so easily. "And you're single because . . ."

"*I'm* a soulless sociopath?" she tried.

"You wish." He chuckled.

"Sometimes," she admitted.

He pointed to her eyes, just as she had pointed to his. "I see you. You're smart and successful, but you're also funny and beautiful."

Her breath caught for a moment. She had no idea how to respond, what to say, or what to do.

"You get things done." His voice deepened with admiration. "You make miracles happen."

"Well." She tucked her hair behind her ear. "I make phone calls. Let's keep this in perspective."

"You must leave a trail of broken hearts wherever you go."

She went silent for a few moments. "Just one."

He let the silence settle in between them. For a minute or two, the only sound was the swiping of the windshield wipers and the droning of the heavy-duty tires against the pavement.

"I grew up in a very stable family in a very stable town with a very lovely life," Holiday finally said. "And I had a very steady boyfriend. Jackson. We got together our junior year of high school and went to the same college and just . . . stayed together."

"You loved him?" Alex asked.

"I . . . yeah." And this was the truth. She *had* loved Jackson as truly and fiercely as only one teenager could love another. "He was a great guy. Sweet and dependable. He was the type of boyfriend everyone would want for their daughter." She lapsed back into silence.

"But?" he prompted.

"We were on different timetables." She struggled to explain. What had happened between them had been so gradual, so nuanced, that it was hard to put into words. "He wanted to settle down as soon as we graduated, you know, get married, buy a house with a white picket fence, the whole deal. And I wanted to see the world before I got a mortgage and a minivan. So we decided to compromise—we were going to save every penny we earned during our last year of college so we could spend the summer after graduation traveling."

He smiled nostalgically, perhaps thinking of his own college days. "Hostels and Eurorail passes?"

"I was so excited." Holiday closed her eyes at the memory. "And then came Christmas Eve. Both of our families got together for dinner, we sang carols and ate cookies, and then . . ." This part still made her physically squirm. "He got down on one knee in front of everyone and proposed."

"And you had *not* been texting him pictures of engagement rings you liked," Alex clarified.

"No. I didn't care about the ring at all. I was too busy trying to figure out what to say. My mouth kept opening and closing, but no words were coming out. And *then*." She still couldn't wrap her mind around this part.

"Uh-oh."

"*Then* he told me that he'd spent our travel fund on the ring." Even after all this time, the memory pricked and prodded her soul. "I burst into tears. In front of our whole families. I still feel horrible about it."

"Why?" Alex sounded mystified. "You didn't do anything wrong."

"He put his heart and soul on the line, and I started crying," she pointed out. "And talking about how much I wanted to see Spain. It was grotesque." She paused to collect herself. "I mean, you should have seen my parents' faces. And *his* parents' faces." And Jackson's face, which of course had been the worst of all. "He loved me. He would have done anything for me, but I couldn't give him what he wanted."

"He wouldn't have gone to Spain for you," Alex pointed out.

"But that's not his fault." As she spoke the words, she realized that she still felt badly about the whole situation. Not for what she had lost, but for the hopes she hadn't fulfilled. "He couldn't help it if he wanted to put down roots and build a stable life for us."

"And you couldn't help if it you didn't," Alex countered.

"Everyone would have been thrilled if I had accepted that proposal." She rattled off the names. "Jackson, his parents, my parents, all our grandparents—"

"But not you," Alex finished for her.

She couldn't refute that.

"And you're kind of important in that equation."

She gave a half-hearted nod. "Since then, though, I've done a great job of granting wishes."

"Everything's easier when it's not your immediate family," he noted.

"Amen. Anyway, by the time the next Christmas rolled around, I had been to Spain," Holiday said. "For work. Went to Toledo to commission a custom-made sword for a client."

"What became of Jackson?" he wanted to know.

"A few years later, he married someone else, and by all accounts, they're very happy. Their house has the best Christmas decorations on the block." She had to smile, thinking of the photos she'd seen on social media. Jackson and his wife really went all out—wreaths and bows and wooden reindeer galore.

"So he survived."

"He survived." And so had all the other guys who had broken up with her when she wasn't available for the flurry of dinners and parties between Thanksgiving and New Year's.

Alex regarded her with an expectant look. "He ended up getting what he wanted, but you still feel bad about it. Have I got that right?"

She flexed her hands on the steering wheel. "It's not that simple."

"Don't you think that you deserve to have your wishes granted too?" he pressed.

"Not at the expense of other people's feelings."

"Like whose?"

Alice and Francie Penewate's, she thought but did not say.

"You're helping all these people find exactly what they want. Who's helping you find what you want?"

"Well." She reached across the console and touched his sleeve. "You are."

He turned toward her, but she snatched her hand away.

"That's enough of everybody's life stories, I think." She knew they were on the verge of having a Moment, but she couldn't handle a Moment. Not right now. "Let's listen to a podcast. A coffee podcast? Your choice."

He glanced down at his wrist where her fingers had rested, then took a second to switch gears.

"Okay." He pulled out his iPhone. "This is great. No one ever wants to do coffee stuff with me. Hang on, let me find the best episode to start with."

As the snow came down harder, the truck's tires gripped the road, and Holiday realized she was actually enjoying the winter weather. She felt warm and cozy, she was hopeful about her chances of securing her target, and she got to spend time with the most interesting guy she'd met in years. He was sharing something with her that he couldn't share with anyone else. Right now, she truly did have everything she wanted.

Too bad it all had to come to an end tomorrow night.

Chapter Twelve

HOLIDAY AND ALEX arrived at the Kilgorff house just before two in the afternoon. Well, "house" was a misnomer in this case—the white Colonial estate with black shutters was festooned with balsam garlands and featured wreaths on every door, including the carriage house, guesthouse, and what appeared to be a stable in the back. A long, brick-paved driveway curved around the house and continued down to the lakeshore.

Holiday squinted. "Is that a boathouse back there by the dock?"

"Looks like stained-glass artistry pays pretty well," Alex said.

"Yeah, apparently, there's a lot of generational wealth from Driscoll, but Crispin is no slouch himself. He made a killing in construction. Or real estate. Something like that," Holiday replied.

"If this guy's so loaded and living the good life out here on the lake, why is he willing to let you rifle through his family heirlooms?" Alex asked. "He doesn't need the money, clearly."

"I don't know." Holiday turned up both palms. "I asked as politely as I could, he seemed cool with it, and my negotiation policy is to stop talking when you get what you want. So I didn't ask a lot of follow-up questions."

Alex regarded the house suspiciously. "Maybe he's got an ulterior motive."

"Maybe he's just a nice guy who's sick of family feuds and is willing to help out a stranger out of the goodness of his heart at Christmas," Holiday countered.

Alex opened the door and climbed out of the truck cab. "Guess we'll find out."

As he and Holiday climbed the stately stone steps leading up to the front door, Holiday pointed to a wooden for-sale sign lying on the porch. "Check it out—he's putting the house on the market. We got here just in time." She reached up and banged the weathered brass door knocker, which was no doubt a priceless antique.

"Welcome, welcome. You must be Miss Smith." Crispin Kilgorff the Third, a portly, mustachioed old-world gentleman in a festive plaid sweater, threw open the front door and ushered Alex and Holiday into the high-ceiling foyer. "Come in."

"Please call me Holly or Holiday." She offered a handshake. "And this is Alex, my, um, assistant."

Alex's eyebrows shot up, but he played along and shook hands. "Pleased to meet you, sir."

"Call me Cris," the homeowner boomed. "Let me take your coats. Can I get you anything to drink? Tea? Coffee? Hot toddy?"

Holiday managed to avoid making eye contact with Alex at the mention of coffee, as they had spent the last hour listening to experts discuss the optimal soil acidity for growing Arabica plants in Brazil. "Water would be lovely, thank you."

"Oh, come now, it's chilly out there. Have something to warm you up. How about hot chocolate?"

"That sounds great," she agreed. "And thank you again for letting me come rummage through your attic."

"Happy to help." Crispin shook his head. "You can't imagine the strife all of my great-grandfather's money and notoriety has caused. Not worth it, at any cost."

"Good karma is coming your way," she assured him. "And don't worry, we'll be quick about it. Out of your hair in an hour, max."

"Oh, you're here!" A petite older woman in a pink tweed suit and a white bouffant click-clacked into the foyer on towering high heels. "Your timing is impeccable." She offered her hand. "I'm Lauren Havers, the real estate agent."

Holiday and Alex's bewilderment must have shown on their faces, because Lauren turned to Crispin with a puzzled expression of her own.

"Aren't these the people you called to clean out the attic?" she asked.

"Indeed, they are." He led the way up the staircase to a small door in the hallway of the second floor. "You two can get started, and I'll send someone up with your cocoa when it's ready."

Alex shot an *I told you so* glance at Holiday, who summoned a smile and tried to decide how to word this delicately. "Mr. Kilgorff, we'll certainly do our best, but I'm not sure we can clean out an entire attic in an hour. And we really need to get back on the road before dusk. But, if you'd like, I'd be happy to arrange for—"

"No need to worry. There's hardly anything left up there." He gave her a hearty clap on the back that nearly knocked her over. "You'll be done in two shakes of a lamb's tail. The packing crates are prepped, and I'll see to it that you have plenty of tape." He opened the door and pulled the chain that turned on a naked lightbulb. A narrow stairway led up into musty darkness.

"Are there any lights up there?" Holiday asked.

"Lots of dormer windows and plenty of daylight left. I'll send up some flashlights and candles, if you like."

The Realtor clapped her hands together. "Splendid! So it's settled." She ushered Alex and Holiday toward the staircase. "Happy hunting!"

The door slammed and Holiday put one foot on the first step, which creaked so loudly that she worried it might snap in two. Her breath stirred up little clouds of dust. "All right," she said to Alex. "Go ahead. Say you told me so."

"Later." He darted around her and sprinted up the stairs. "Right now, we have work to do."

"Sorry." She followed him up, clutching the banister. "This isn't what you signed up for."

"Eh, it's cleaning out an attic. How hard could it be?"

Holiday mounted the top of the stairs and surveyed the vast, shadowed landscape of boxes and furniture draped in sheets. She planted her feet and put her hands on her hips. "You're right. We can do this."

"We'll make a plan and execute," he said. "Start at one side and work through section by section. Come on." He grabbed her hand. "Let's start at this wall."

She squeezed his hand back, whereupon both of them immediately pulled away. "The first thing we need is adequate lighting. Here." She turned on her phone's flashlight and balanced it atop a pile of wooden crates.

He pulled a pocketknife out of his coat and started slicing into cardboard containers. "Extraneous packing material can go over here." He yanked out some tissue paper and tossed it in the corner. "And we'll need something inspiring to listen to. What's your poison?"

"It's December twenty-third. Christmas music all the way." Holiday sliced open the box next to his and pulled out a mystery object wrapped in an old towel.

"Modern or traditional?" he asked.

"Mix it up."

With a few swipes on his phone screen, Nat King Cole started crooning about chestnuts roasting and what could have been drudgery turned into the ultimate scavenger hunt.

Twenty minutes later, they'd unearthed antique books, two weather-warped cellos, a passel of broken skis, an old-timey spinning wheel, a dozen pairs of ladies' shoes from the 1950s, and a roll-top desk that, as Alex put, "was probably where Edgar Allan Poe wrote 'The Raven.'" They had huge mugs of cocoa, and they had Mariah Carey and Brenda Lee on the playlist. What they didn't have—at least not yet—was any sign of stained glass.

Holiday nibbled her lower lip. "I hope there's something

good in the next stack of boxes. He said that his grandfather used this attic as a studio for drawing and design. I mean, there has to be *something*, right?"

"There's stained glass up here." Alex sounded one hundred percent confident.

"How can you be so sure?" she asked.

"Because I refuse to accept the alternative." He gave her a wry smile, and she recognized a stubborn spark of determination in his eyes. It was the same spark she experienced whenever someone told her a deadline was too tight or a challenge was too insurmountable.

"Pass the knife, please." She knelt down and held out her palm. "I feel lucky."

"Roll us some sevens." He pressed the handle of the pocketknife into her palm. "Daddy needs a new—I mean an old—stained-glass star."

Holiday sucked in her breath, cut through the packing tape, and unwound a yard of yellowed muslin from . . . "What is this?" She held the object up to the light. "A hammer?" Her excitement gave way to disappointment.

He examined the small, double-edged tool. "A miniature pickaxe?"

And then her research came flooding back. "Wait, I know! This is a cutting tool for stained glass." She reached into the box and pulled out another metal tool. "And this is a cutting wheel. Ladies and gentlemen, we've reached the stained-glass portion of this afternoon's entertainment."

As the scent of cinnamon and vanilla drifted up from the kitchen, they ripped through the next box in the pile. In a matter of minutes, they amassed rusty cans labeled "potash," "lime," and "sand," as well as long strips of lead and wooden laths.

"Well," Holiday said, "the good news is that we'll probably be able to make a glass star ourselves by the time we're done up here. All we need is the kiln and a few instructional YouTube videos."

And then Alex discovered the lamp. Hidden under a dirty drop cloth, Holiday had assumed the dome-shaped item was a birdcage, but no. When the cloth was whisked away, she knew exactly what she was looking at.

"I can't believe it," she whispered, reaching out, but afraid to touch the intricate glass mosaic of red, blue, green, and gold. "It's a Driscoll Davidson Nasturnium table lamp. Do you know how much these are going for at art house auctions?"

Alex studied the leaded glass shade, which depicted intricate blossoms and fern fronds. "How do you know it's legit?"

"Hang on, bring the flashlight over." Holiday turned the lamp over to examine the base. Upon lifting the cap, she could see a heavy metal ring that appeared to be made of lead. "So far, so good."

Then she examined the slight greenish patina that had spread across the base of the lamp. Finally, she scrutinized the lamp knobs and the etchings carved into the base.

"I'd need to take this to a professional appraiser to be certain, but all signs point to this being the real thing. Not to mention, we found it in the actual glassmaker's attic."

They found two more lamps and a vase before they hit

the Christmas stockpile.

"Red alert!" Holiday cried as she sifted through a cardboard box spotted with mildew. "We have an ornament!" She held up a delicate glass globe designed to look like bright-red peonies in bloom.

She handed it off the Alex and reached back into the box. "And another!" This one was a tableau featuring a white swan with a red scarf against a blue background.

"So close, but so far." Alex grimaced in agony.

The attic door creaked open and Crispin's voice drifted up from the hallway. "Do you two need anything up there?"

"No!" they yelled in unison.

Holiday cleared her throat. "I mean, no thank you, Mr. Kilgorff. How kind of you to check on us."

"All right, then, I'll leave you to it." The door clicked closed.

She flattened one box and prepared to open the next. "Alex, would you care to do the honors?"

"I would, thank you." He sliced through the twine and tape. She nestled into his shoulder to get a better view. He pulled out an item so distinctive that even wads of tissue paper couldn't disguise it.

"It's a star," she murmured.

He unwrapped it with the care and caution one might afford to a ticking time bomb . . . and pulled out a gorgeous green glass star.

His whole body slumped in disappointment. "Right shape, right size, wrong color. My mom's was red and gold."

"Keep going," she commanded.

He was staring at the green glass. "If I got truly desperate, maybe I could just take out the green glass and have a glassmaker fill in the frame with different colors."

"No need." She plunged both hands into the box and pulled out a blue-and-silver star.

"It'd be hard to replicate the swirl effect, though." He was still studying the green piece. "I'm pretty sure all the lead they used in these is outlawed now."

"Red and gold, you say?" Holiday spun around with a new piece in hand. "Like this one?"

Alex's expression told her all she needed to know. His was the face of a man informed that he had received a last-moment pardon from death row . . . or from having to tell his mother that he'd broken her favorite Christmas keepsake.

"That's it. That's it!" His smile faded. "I think."

"Okay, well, let's cross-reference with our primary source." Holiday's tone was reassuring. "Show me the photo of the original."

He went through his phone until he found it.

She took the phone and the star to the window and examined every centimeter of the tree topper, from the thickness of the lead and the etchings on the inside of the bottom to the ripples in the glass. "This is it," she confirmed. "Or at least, it's as close as we're ever going to get."

He peered over her shoulder. She could feel his breath on her neck and the warmth of his skin radiating into hers. "Where are the differences?"

"Well, look at the whorl of the red glass here." She ran her index finger over the pattern on one pointed panel. "It's the same color as the one in your picture, but the texture is different."

He got even closer to get a better look. "She won't notice that." He paused. "Do you think she'll notice that?"

"I've never met your mom, so I can't say." She tilted her head. "Ninety-nine percent of people could never tell the difference. Do you think your mother is part of that eagle-eyed one percent?"

"She got her glasses prescription changed recently." He sounded hopeful. "Maybe she's not as detail-oriented as she used to be."

"She's got no reason to suspect a swap, right?" She resisted the urge to lean back against him. "Just put it up on top of the tree as quickly as possible and change the subject."

"I'll have Paul provide a distraction," Alex said. "He can spill cheese dip all over her couch or something."

"Genius." Holiday allowed herself a moment to savor their triumph. This feeling never got old. She had finagled her way through black ice, Wi-Fi outages, sabotaged family trees, and crappy two-wheel drive to deliver exactly what she'd promised to Alex. Which meant that she could now deliver him to Alice and Francie Penewate. Which meant that she could deliver on her own promise to her family to finally join them for snowflake-patterned jammies and cinnamon rolls while they rummaged through their stockings.

Note to self: Buy stocking stuffers for parents and sister.

She detected a tinge of pink in the sky. "We better hurry. It's getting late."

They unpacked and sorted out the rest of the attic's contents with ruthless speed and efficiency. All items were categorized into one of three designations: trash, donate, or priceless works of art. They hauled the trash down to the bins in the backyard and called out for Mr. Kilgorff.

"Done?" He marveled at the smudges of dirt on their hands, faces, and clothes as they returned to the foyer. "That must have been quite a mess up there. Did you find any good glass?"

"We found several," she confirmed. "Vases, lamps, and ornaments. And even a few tree-toppers." She pointed out the red-and-gold piece she'd placed carefully on the end table. "This one is exactly what we need."

"I'm so pleased to hear it! Finally, something positive will come out of this nasty family rift."

She made a point of shifting her weight and checking her watch. "And I noticed that it's getting a bit late, so I was hoping we could settle up and be on our way."

Alex nodded. "How much do you want for it?"

"That star?" The old man tapped his fingers on the tabletop. "I'm not sure it's possible to put a price on that."

"It is," Holiday assured him. "I spent some time looking up auction house listings from the last two years."

"I get it," Alex added. "I'm in no position to negotiate. You tell me what you want, and I'll send it your way right now. Do you take Venmo? Zelle? Or I can just pay cash."

Crispin was stroking his white beard. "I think we can all agree that I have more than my fair share of filthy lucre."

Holiday froze. Was he going to *give* them a Driscoll Davidson original? For free? Talk about Christmas miracles.

But Alex was having none of it. "Sir, you saved my hide by letting me clean out your attic. I'm happy to pay market price."

Crispin continued to ponder his options. "As I said, I don't need the money."

"Fine." A note of impatience crept into Alex's voice. "I'll make a donation to the charity of your choice."

"That's a splendid suggestion. I'm a big supporter of our local children's service agency," Crispin said. "I throw a party for them every December. In fact, I'm heading down to the county club to host the cocktail hour in just a bit."

"Then I'll write a check to them." Alex pulled out his wallet. "Just tell me the name of the agency."

"And have a great time at the party." Holiday headed for the coat closet.

"Slow down, both of you. We have a bit of a situation here and I might need your help." Crispin hurried back to the kitchen, where Holiday could hear a flurry of muffled voices.

Moments later, he burst back into the siting room.

"Smell that? My staff has been baking sugar cookies for hours. There must be hundreds of them!"

Alex had reached the end of his graciousness. "Sir, we have to leave, so I can either pay you now or have my accountant wire you money tomorrow. Whichever you prefer."

"As it turns out, a few of the catering assistants can't make it to the party tonight," Crispin said. "They came down with a nasty cold and I can't have anyone sneezing and coughing all over the cookies."

Holiday and Alex exchanged glances and waited him out.

"We're short-staffed now," Crispin concluded. "And the decorate-your-own cookie station isn't going to run itself. That's where you come in."

Chapter Thirteen

HOLIDAY RACKED HER brain for a moment before replying. "We'd love to, of course, but we're not licensed caterers."

"You don't need to be a professional chef to sling some frosting." Crispin chuckled at the thought. "You can put on a uniform and blend right in."

"Even if that's true, we really have to get going before the weather gets any worse. It's a long drive back to Maine and I have a bad track record with snowstorms." She ran her hand through her hair. "But have no fear, I'm very good at logistics. I can scrounge up some replacements in the next hour or so."

"No." The old man's expression was serene and utterly certain. "I'd like you to do it."

"But . . ." Holiday started.

"Why?" Alex finished.

"Because Christmas is a time for reflection and giving." Crispin smiled kindly at Alex. "Writing a check isn't a sacrifice for you. I can relate to that—giving you a piece of my great-grandfather's glasswork isn't any sacrifice to me. So I've made a point of giving something more treasured than money—time and effort."

Holiday wanted to point out that she was not obscenely rich and should therefore be excluded from this narrative, but she couldn't abandon her teammate. Not when the finish line was so close.

She glanced at the grandfather clock in the hallway. "What time does this shindig start?"

"Crafts and games begin promptly at six," Crispin said.

She turned to Alex. "What do you think? Will we be able to drive all the way back to Alemos tonight?"

"I don't see that we have a choice."

Crispin clapped his hands together. "Now you're in the spirit!"

She turned to Crispin with schoolmarm sternness. "We will give you two hours of cookie decorating. But that's it. We have miles to go before we sleep."

"The children will be thrilled," he said.

"I promise you that we'll be the best cookie-decorating assistants that ever assisted." She leveled her index finger at him. "But we're out of here at the stroke of eight o'clock and we're taking your great-grandfather's star with us."

"Eight thirty?" he countered.

"One hundred and twenty minutes. No more, no less." She planted her hands on her hips. "Eight sharp. Take it or leave it."

He relented with a laugh. "You drive a hard bargain, Miss Smith. Let me go share the good news with the catering team."

When they were alone, Alex turned to her. "I can't believe this."

"What else could I do?" she demanded. "We have no other options and he knows it. Besides, what kind of monster says no to helping children at Christmas?"

Alex waved this away. "No, I can't believe you forgot to ask the most important question."

She frowned. "Which is?"

"What are the uniforms like?"

"DON'T SAY ONE word," Alex warned as he stepped out of the powder room.

"Well, well, well." Holiday tried and failed to hide her grin as she beheld Alex Sappier—titan of tech, mountain man of Maine, coffee connoisseur—rocking a Santa hat, green turtleneck and pants, and red-and-green-striped elf shoes with jingle bells dangling from the curly toes. "It's a lot of look, but you're pulling it off."

"It's all fun and games until you have to suit up." He held the powder room door for her, where her version of the elf outfit awaited.

"I'm looking forward to it." She squared her shoulders as she prepared to face her sartorial fate. "It's for the kids."

"Keep telling yourself that."

And she did, repeating the words over and over as she wriggled her stocking feet into ill-fitting elf shoes and tried to arrange the Santa hat at the most alluring angle on her head.

But after a few moments, she had to admit the truth— there *was* no alluring way to wear a Santa hat. Santa hats didn't lend themselves to coy flirtation or sultry glances. So she rummaged through her purse, dug out the red lipstick she hardly ever used, and decided to lean into the "jolly old elf" side of her persona.

"I make this look good." She threw open the powder room door with aplomb. "Rustle up the flying reindeer and let's get going."

Alex's gaze fixed on her mouth.

"What?" She pressed her lips together, suddenly self-conscious. "Too much? Does it clash with the hat?"

He snapped out of it and shook his head. "No, it looks good. I just . . . Let me go warm up the car."

"The caterers have the cookies, right?" she called after him.

"Cris said they're already there setting everything up. All we have to do is show up and starting doling out icing and sprinkles."

She leveled her gaze at Alex. "You call him Cris now?"

"I'm on a first-name basis with all people who force me to dress up like Father Christmas." He strode out the front door and into the gusting night wind.

Cris himself strode into the foyer, now attired in a perfectly tailored tuxedo, featuring a bowtie with blinking red and green lights. "Miss Smith, you look splendid!"

She struck a pose under the massive, sparkling chandelier. "Thanks. It's straight off the runway from the North Pole. Elf couture."

"I want you to know that I truly appreciate this." He straightened his bedazzled bow tie. "I know that you and your boyfriend probably had plans tonight, but it means the world to me to do this for the children every year."

"It's our pleasure," she assured him. "You've been incredibly kind and generous." She cleared her throat. "And, um, he's not my boyfriend."

"Oh no?" He gave her a conspiratorial wink. "I saw the way you two were looking at each other."

Her entire face felt as though it were spontaneously combusting. "No, no. We're just coworkers. Kind of."

"Far be it from me to argue with a lovely lady doing me a favor," he said. "It's nearly time to leave. You're not driving, are you?"

She glanced out at the darkening sky and icy pavement. "I think I'll leave that to my coworker."

"Splendid." He crossed the living room to the limestone-topped wet bar. "Then have a cocktail with me."

"Oh, I couldn't."

"You can. You must!" he insisted. "What's your poison? Bourbon? A Manhattan?" Upon seeing her expression, he switched tactics. "May I tempt you with a Mistletoe Martini?"

She felt her resolve weakening. "I don't know what that is, but it sounds good."

"It is," he assured her. "Vodka, elderflower liqueur, fresh cranberries, mint leaves . . ."

"Hang on." Holiday entered the ingredient list into her phone to access later. "That sounds heavenly, but I can't handle these shoes, a bunch of kids, and dozens of cookies if I'm tipsy."

"A workaholic, I see." He sighed as he gave the wet bar one last, longing look.

Holiday nodded. "You don't know the half of it."

"All right then, an Irish coffee for the road." He held up his hand to stave off any protests. "Don't worry, I'll go easy on the whisky."

"Just the tiniest splash." She watched as he prepared the drink in a high-end, stainless steel, double-walled travel mug. "Make sure I give that back to you at the end of the evening."

He waved this away. "Keep it. A token of my appreciation."

"But you already gave us the tree topper," she protested. "We can never repay you."

He pressed the mug into her hand. "See you at the country club. Do you need directions?"

The front door opened and Alex stepped back into the foyer. "I thought we were in a hurry to get going?" He blinked when he noticed Crispin's tux and tie.

"We're getting some coffee for the road," Holiday told Alex. "Mine is spiked, but you should have some plain old caffeine."

Alex regarded the travel mug suspiciously. "No offense, but I'm kind of a coffee snob."

Holiday turned to Crispin. "You can take the 'kind of' out of that sentence."

Crispin looked delighted to hear this. "A fellow java enthusiast! You've come to the right place. You must try this roast from Panama. It's got opening notes of jasmine and white grape and finishes with a rich cocoa flavor."

Holiday furrowed her brow. "Are we talking about coffee or fine wine?"

Both men ignored her and launched into an intense conversation about the merits of African versus South American blends. After the term "dynamic complexity" was bandied about, Holiday felt compelled to remind them:

"Gentlemen. The children await. Shall we?" She put a hand on each man's shoulder and ushered them to the door.

"All right, all right." Crispin nodded at Alex over Holiday's head. "I have a rare blend from Costa Rica that you simply must try. Let me give you a few beans to take with you."

"*Boys.*" Holiday dragged them both by the sleeve and shoved them out the front door. "We are leaving now." She abandoned her insulated mug and turned to Alex as she mentally revised the driving plans. "Give me your keys. I'll take your truck, and you can ride with Crispin and talk coffee, and meet me there."

Alex handed them over and headed toward Crispin's garage, talking and gesticulating wildly about the marvels of Costa Rica's acidic soil and north-facing slopes.

Holiday hurried into the truck, turned on the ignition, and cranked up the heat. She entered the country club into her GPS system and put her foot on the brake, whereupon she realized that driving in jingly elf shoes was going to be even harder than driving in stiletto heels.

Never one to back down from a challenge, she flipped back the white puffball atop her Santa hat and eased the truck into reverse.

"If I can handle this truck in these shoes, I can handle anything."

"DON'T FREAK OUT," Alex said as he settled into the wooden folding chair next to Holiday's. "We can handle this."

"How did you know I was freaking out?" Holiday surveyed the spread of culinary delights displayed on the table before them—naked cut-out sugar cookies, pastry bags filled with colored icing, nonpareils, crystal sugar, sprinkles, and gold and silver sugar pearls. "I love cookies. I love kids. But I don't actually know anything about cookies or kids."

He patted her back. And left his hand resting between her shoulder blades. She tried not to notice it, but it was all she could feel.

"What's to know?" he scoffed. "All we have to do is keep the cookies and icing coming."

She glanced toward the massive double doors that were about to swing open and unleash a throng of children who were already amped on sugar and seasonal anticipation. "But what if they want to talk to us? I don't know how to talk to children."

"Neither do I, but I guarantee they won't want to talk." His hand was still on her back. She could feel the warmth of his palm through her shirt. "They just want to glonk some frosting on a cookie, shove it in their mouths, and go on their way."

She narrowed her eyes at him. "I think you seriously underestimate the sophistication of today's youths."

"I'm confident in my prediction. And I say that as someone who's made a lot of money from making predictions."

The doors flew open and there was no more time to freak out—the youths were upon them. Dozens of chubby-cheeked cherubs decked out in sweater vests and velvet dresses swarmed the cookie-decorating station. Most of them snatched up cookies and frosting and ignored the adults entirely. But others . . .

"What's your name?" a little girl with ringlets and a plaid hair bow demanded.

Holiday smiled. "Holiday."

The little girl shook her head. "No, I mean your *real* name."

Holiday could see Alex stifling a laugh. "That is my real name."

"No, it's not," the girl insisted. "What's your name when you're not pretending to be an elf?"

Holiday had to stifle a laugh herself. "Listen, kid, I'll level with you. I'm not a real elf. You've got me dead to rights there. I'm a North Pole imposter. But Holiday is my real name. I swear on this sugar cookie."

A boy who looked to be eleven or twelve jumped into the conversation. "Are you named after the Madonna song?"

"My parents would die if they heard you ask that," Holiday told him. "They weren't big Madonna fans."

Alex leaned over. "Aren't you too young to know who Madonna is?"

The kid straightened his pocket square. "I can use the internet."

"I'm named after a jazz singer," Holiday continued. "Named Billie Holiday."

"They named their baby girl after a boy?" The little ringleted girl was aghast.

Before Holiday could explain, another child sidled up and pointed first at Alex, then at Holiday. "Are you guys married?"

"No, you dum-dum," a freckled redhead piped up. "Look, they don't have any rings on."

"You can be married without rings," the first child shot back.

"No, you can't."

"Yeah, you can." The first kid looked ready to push up his sleeves and start a brawl.

"We're not married," Holiday said. "Now. Who would like to decorate this snowman cookie?"

The children glanced at the cookie for half a second before resuming their interrogation. The redhead rounded on Alex. "What's your name?"

"Your real name, not your elf name," Ringlets hastened to add.

"Alexander Sappier." He kept a completely straight face. "Executive assistant for Kris Kringle and Associates since approximately four p.m. today. Would you care to review my CV?"

The dapper young gentleman with the pocket square ignored all this and tilted his head toward Holiday. "Is she your girlfriend?"

Alex managed to hang on to his poker face. "No."

The kids leaned in. "But do you like her?"

"Like, *like* her like her?"

Holiday busied herself with piping yellow spindles onto a star-shaped cookie.

Alex cleared his throat. "I have the right to remain silent."

"No, you don't." The little girl stuck out her bottom lip.

"I have the right to an attorney."

"You guys!" Holiday physically put cookies into the children's hands. "Look at all this frosting. Come on, let's see who can make the most awesome cookie."

The children glanced down at the cookies, but made no move to start decorating.

"Winner gets to wear these elf shoes," she threw in. This elicited some half-hearted mumbling.

She looked at Alex. He looked back at her.

"Decorate cookies with the kids, they said. It'll be fun, they said." She laughed.

"I haven't seen a cross-examination like that since I sat in on an FDA drug review meeting." He actually had a bead of sweat on his forehead.

"You said you'd do anything to get that star for your mom," she reminded him.

"Yeah, but that was intense. I had no idea kids were so inquisitive these days."

Holiday nibbled on a bell-shaped cookie. "Oh, I'd bet you were a pretty inquisitive little kid yourself."

Neither of them mentioned all the talk about girlfriends and *liking* liking each other, but the topic remained between them, as massive and awkward as a moose hunkered down at the table.

"Here." Holiday intervened before the girl with the ringlets squirted green icing all over her dress. "Let me help."

"Thanks." The girl screwed up her face in concentration as she attempted to pipe a perfectly formed wreath. "I really want to wear those shoes."

Holiday beckoned her in and whispered, "Check in with me when this is over and we'll make it happen."

The girl smiled. "You're nice." She lifted her chin toward Alex. "He *should* marry you."

Holiday smiled back and swallowed a sigh. "We'll take that under advisement."

Thankfully, the conversation progressed to less emotionally loaded topics, such as TikTok, video games, and Pokemon. Alex and Holiday decided to display a tray of cookies so that guests could vote for their favorites, but orderly voting proved difficult as the kids kept eating their masterpieces before they could be displayed for more than a few minutes.

"You're getting really good at this," Holiday complimented Alex as he advised a kindergartener on the best technique for creating spindles on a snowflake.

"Right back at you." He studied the tinsel she'd created on a cookie tree with red icing and silver sugar pearls. "By the time this is over, we'll be ready to go on one of those holiday baking shows."

"Two overachieving workaholics, ten dozen cookies, and five hundred pounds of frosting," she said.

"That show sells itself." He handed the cookie back to the kindergartener. "What do you think?"

The five-year-old scrutinized the zillionaire tech guru's handiwork. "Eh. It's okay. Needs more sprinkles."

Alex passed the sugar crystals. "Can't argue with that."

"You must be relieved to have that tree topper in hand," she said. "Christmas is saved."

"You did it." He sat back and gazed at the sugar-fueled chaos all around them. "In the weirdest way possible."

"Not to brag, but that's kind of my specialty." She reached over and flicked the white puffball attached to his Santa hat. "Never a dull moment."

"Paul wants me to pass along his gratitude." Alex pulled out his phone and read Paul's text verbatim: "'Tell H she is a miracle worker.' Happy crying emoji. 'Mom will let us live to see another Christmas. Now you do your part and sweep the hot girl from high school off her feet.'"

"That's sweet." But the enthusiasm faded from Holiday's voice. They had indeed arrived at the "sweep the hot girl from high school off her feet" portion of this bargain. The portion where she had to turn Alex over to a stranger.

The sucky portion.

And yes, by all accounts, this stranger was a bright, beautiful, good-hearted woman who had appreciated everything Alex had to offer long before he became a big-bucks big shot. But somehow that didn't lessen the sting; it actually made it sharper.

"I know I wasn't crazy about this idea when you first pitched it," Alex continued. "But I'm a man of my word. You get what's-her-name to Alemos Island by tomorrow afternoon, and I'll go from jolly elf to Prince Charming like that." He snapped his fingers. "I'm all in."

"Thank you." She plastered the smile back on her face. "Let's get this cookie competition back on track, shall we?"

But before she could proceed with reestablishing rules and regulations, an announcer leaped onto the dais by the gleaming floor-to-ceiling window and bellowed, "Attention, all! I've just been informed that Santa has arrived."

Every child's head whipped around as the MC made his way through the activity booths to the Christmas tree towering by the fireplace. "He'll be here momentarily to hand out gifts and good tidings. Gather 'round, one and all, gather 'round!"

What happened next was more of a pint-sized stampede than a "gathering 'round." Children dropped their cookies and bolted for the tree, slipping and squealing as they ran.

Alex's eyes widened. "I hope they gave Santa riot gear."

Holiday sat back to watch the scene, delight bubbling up within her. This was what made her feel most alive—the unbridled enthusiasm that came from hope and togetherness and belief in magic. That's when she noticed that one little girl had remained at the cookie station, her gaze fixed on Holiday's footwear.

"Why are you—of course!" Holiday clapped her hand to her forehead as she remembered her promise to the ringleted rascal. "You're waiting to try on these shoes?"

The child nodded, her expression wistful. "That's what I want for Christmas."

"Well, it's your lucky day. I happen to be a professional wish granter." Holiday slipped out of the jingling elf shoes, leaving her clad in thin gray socks. "Try these on and see how you like them."

The girl sat down on the carpet, doffed her black patent Mary Janes, and wriggled her toes into the shoes. She stood up and took two careful steps, then announced, "They fit perfectly."

This was clearly a lie in the literal sense, as the child's feet were swimming in the slippers, but Holiday discerned the girl's underlying statement. The shoes *were* a perfect fit, in terms of her style, her dreams, her self-image.

"Keep 'em." Holiday grinned.

The girl's mouth dropped open. "For real?"

"My shift's over and I wear the finest designer high-heeled boots when I'm working at the North Pole." She turned to Alex and informed him, "Santa set me up with a corner office with a private bathroom and uninterrupted views of the tundra."

"Nice." He helped himself to a sugar cookie. "Do you get good health benefits?"

"The best. Plus vision and dental and vet insurance." She winked at the little girl. "For my pet polar bear."

The child scoffed. "You don't have a pet polar bear." She paused. "Do you?"

"Santa runs a pet-friendly workplace," Holiday assured her.

"What's your polar bear's name?"

"Um." Holiday cleared her throat. "Shackleton."

"Wrong pole," Alex said.

"No one likes a know-it-all," Holiday informed him loftily. "Young woman, you have a wonderful night and wear those shoes in good health."

The girl shuffled off, practically skating in her attempt to keep her feet in the shoes and jingling all the way.

Holiday noticed Crispin watching them from a few yards away. "You were right," she told him. "The cookies were a hit and these kids definitely needed supervision."

"Thank you, both of you." He appeared to be misty-eyed. "You're very good sports."

"Our pleasure," Alex assured him.

"I gave away the elf shoes," Holiday confessed. "I probably should have asked first, but she wanted them so badly—I can relate, I'm kind of a shoe enthusiast myself. I'll pay you back or talk to the caterer, whatever you need."

"The whole point of this party is to provide a magical, over-the-top experience." Crispin looked delighted. "Don't give it a second thought. And you're free to go now, if you like. You've donated your one hundred and twenty minutes."

"It's been . . . really something," Alex said. "But yeah, we'd better get going. It'll be a long drive back with this weather."

"And I have a lot to do tomorrow," Holiday added.

"Ah yes, Christmas Eve." Crispin brushed off his sleeve. "I'm sure you're looking forward to spending time with your own family."

"Yes, I am," Holiday said firmly. "Because I'm going to make it home in time for Christmas morning."

Alex squeezed her shoulder. "You'll be home in plenty of time. All you have to do is make the introductions at six p.m. and hit the road. I'll handle the rest."

"Drive safely," Crispin urged before he rejoined the festivities.

Holiday took a moment to savor the laughter and music and smell of fresh cookies . . . then she turned her attention to a more practical matter—her shoeless feet. "My boots are out in your truck. Would you mind running out and grabbing them for me?"

He shook his head. "As you would say, we're on a schedule." He turned around and crouched down. "Hop on."

She wrapped her arms around his shoulders and he lifted her and took off, striding through the lobby, across the portico, and down to the parking lot. He didn't falter on the stairs or slip on the ice. He kept on, sure and steady, until he'd reached the truck, opened the passenger side door, and deposited her on the leather seat. "Full service, all the way."

She scootched back and tried to ignore how flustered she felt. "Is this your subtle way of telling me you want to drive?"

"Nope." He walked around the truck cab, slid into the driver's seat, and started the ignition. "This is."

Chapter Fourteen

ALEX STEERED THE pickup truck through the snowbanks edging the parking area and the winding gravel road leading up to the highway. "That was wild. I haven't been to a Christmas party in years. Ever since . . ."

Holiday leaned in. "Ever since what?"

He tried to sidestep this. "And I've *definitely* never been to a Christmas party like this one."

"How can you have not been to a holiday party in years?" She located her boots in the back seat and pulled them on. "You must have thrown lots of shindigs for your employees back in your tech bro days."

"I wrote the checks, I didn't actually go," he clarified. "Tech bros tend to be antisocial."

"Well, now you know what you're missing."

He stopped the truck at a red light, turned his head, and looked her in the eye. "I sure do."

She stared back at him for a moment, her breath caught in her throat. The only sound was the hum of air through the heating vents and the soft rustle of snow falling on a wet windshield.

The light turned green. No one moved.

And then the glow of headlights appeared in the rear

window and a car honked.

Holiday had no idea what to say as they sped along under the heavy, starless night sky. Her phone chimed to break the silence as a text from Janine popped up: *Did you find the glass grail?*

Holiday typed back: *Yes. We had to spend hours cleaning out an attic straight out of Hoarders, but we struck gold at the end.*

Janine responded immediately: *"We"?!? Who's "we"?*

Holiday texted: *I'll tell you later.*

Janine: *Yeah, you will. If someone else doesn't tell me first. Word travels fast around here.*

Holiday tried to change the subject: *Did you find a good gift for your mom?*

Janine: *Not yet. "We" didn't happen to find any cross-stitched samplers up in that attic, did we?*

Holiday: *No, but if you want an antique spinning wheel straight out of Sleeping Beauty, I've got you covered.*

She glanced up from her phone as she felt the truck slow. "What's up?"

"I'm not sure." Alex turned on the hazard lights and prepared to pull over to the side of the highway, where a car was parked, also flashing hazard lights.

Holiday clutched the shoulder strap of her seatbelt. "Hang on—you're stopping?"

"Yeah."

"What? No! This is how people get stranded by the side of the road."

"I'm not going to just drive by. What if they need help?"

"What if they just accidentally threw an incredibly rare vinyl record on the highway and we run over it and ruin their hopes and dreams?" she blurted out.

He took a moment to process this. "What?"

"It can happen. Take it from me."

Alex opened his mouth, presumably to pose a follow-up question, then thought better of it. "I'll take my chances." He eased the truck to a stop alongside the snowbank towering next to the breakdown lane and opened the driver's-side door.

Holiday opened the passenger side door, only to realize that the snowbank was blocking her in. So she scrambled over the center console and out the driver's-side door.

By the time she made it out of the truck cab, Alex had already struck up a conversation with the other motorist through the window of the car. Holiday held up her forearm to shield her eyes from the fat, wet snowflakes pelting down and joined him.

The motorist turned out to be a petite young woman with a sleeping infant strapped into a car seat. As Holiday came into earshot, she heard the woman explaining to Alex that, "I really appreciate your stopping, but I'm okay. I didn't realize how much snow we'd be getting and I just pulled over to put on my tire chains."

Alex nodded. "I'd be happy to assist."

The woman's expression was strained. "No, no, that's okay, I can—" Her face relaxed as she spotted Holiday. "Oh, hi."

"Hi!" Holiday gave her a reassuring smile, then explained to Alex, "She's trying to figure out if you're a serial killer."

He accepted this with equanimity. "Fair enough."

Holiday peeked over the driver's shoulder at the baby, who sported a knitted cap with bear ears. "How old?"

"Eight months." The woman rubbed her forehead with the heel of her hand. "Finally fell asleep after crying for twenty miles straight. We're on my way to my brother's house. I didn't check the weather because I'm an idiot."

"Or because you've been sleep-deprived for eight months and your little angel was crying in your ear for twenty miles," Holiday suggested.

The woman smiled. "Either way, I have tire chains in the trunk, so I'm good to go."

"Well, since we're here, we'd love to help you with the tire chains," Holiday said. "It's really more a two- or three-person job anyway."

"Really?" Relief washed over the woman's face. "I don't want to trouble you."

"No trouble." Holiday rapped the top of the car. "We do this all the time."

The woman popped the trunk latch, revealing a tangled loop of chains and cables. Alex straightened out the lines and asked Holiday, "Have you ever put on snow chains?"

"Not once," she replied cheerfully.

"So you don't, in fact, 'do this all the time'?"

"No, but I have a can-do attitude and access to the internet, so I'm sure I could figure it out if needed. Plus, I'm guessing that you actually *do* do this all the time."

"It's been years," he admitted. "Four-wheel drive is a thing."

"Well, if we get cracking and cooperate, I'm sure we can this squared away before that baby in the bear hat wakes up." Holiday brushed her hair out of her eyes. "Where do we start?"

Working together, they managed to center the tire chains behind each rear wheel, connect the appropriate chains and cables, and tighten the loops within fifteen minutes.

"Voila!" Holiday stood up and admired their handiwork. "That looks great! And we hardly even cursed."

"*I* didn't curse at all," Alex corrected her.

"Right, so if you average it out, *we* only cursed a little bit."

Holiday knelt down to reexamine the cable connections while Alex instructed the driver to ease the car into gear and pull forward a few feet. Suddenly, the car's front wheels spun, spraying snow, icy gravel, and sand into Holiday's face.

"Sorry!" the driver cried. "Sorry. I think the bumper is stuck on something."

"No worries." Holiday wiped a coating of ice and dirt from her face. She could feel a frigid trickle of melting snow seeping down her back. While Alex checked the bumper situation and urged the motorist to try again with a lighter touch on the gas pedal, Holiday realized that she was going to be soaking from the inside out.

"Thank you both so much." The driver looked to be near tears as she started to roll her window back up in preparation for getting back on the road.

BETH KENDRICK

"Our pleasure," Alex assured her. "And remember, keep it under twenty-five miles per hour, stay off bare asphalt, and try not to stop too abruptly."

"Got it." Amid a chorus of cries amid all three of them to stay safe and take care, the driver and her still-snoozing baby headed down the highway.

"I RESCIND MY earlier comments about ruining people's hopes and dreams," Holiday said as Alex started up the truck. The snowfall was so dense and accumulating so quickly that they had to crawl along the road with their hazard lights on. "That was really kind of you to stop and help. It warms my heart."

"Are you sure? Because you seem like you're freezing to me."

"Don't look at me . . . keep your eyes on the road!"

"I don't have to look," he shot back. "I can hear your teeth chattering."

Holiday harrumphed at this exaggeration, but she couldn't deny that the faceful of snow had melted into a full-body ice bath, which had seeped into the lining of her coat. Her arms and torso were encased in cold, sodden fabric speckled with sand and salt crystals.

"I'm not cold," she insisted.

"Uh-huh." He turned up the heat.

Approximately two miles later, he pulled the truck over. At first, Holiday assumed that the road conditions had

140

finally become impassable, but Alex shrugged out of his jacket, passed it to her, and resumed driving.

"What are you doing? I can't take this from you." She pushed the coat back toward him, but he was having none of it.

"Put it on," he commanded. "Or we'll have to stop at the ER when you get hypothermia."

"You just worry about your own self, buddy."

"Sorry, that's not my way." He smiled. "Plus, if you're out of commission with hypothermia, who will drag the dream-date scenario over the finish line?"

"Paul?"

He shuddered at the thought. "Paul's idea of a dream date is ice fishing at four in the morning and frying the catch up for breakfast. I doubt that's what your client has in mind."

She sighed and relented, knowing even as she slipped out of her waterlogged jacket and into the dry coat prewarmed with his body heat that he was right. Her responsibility was to deliver him up with a big, red, metaphorical bow to someone else who could never put snow chains on tires with him the way she could.

It was *not* her responsibility to duck her head and inhale the fresh, woodsy smell that lingered on the collar of his jacket. But she did it anyway.

Finally, as they crossed the state line between New Hampshire and Maine, the snowfall abated. Holiday felt her whole body relax. She hadn't been aware of how much tension she'd been holding.

"Oh good." Alex sounded relieved too. "The longer it's clear, the better chance that the bridge to the island will be open by the time we get there."

"How often do they close the bridge?" Holiday asked.

"As often as they need to. It depends on the weather conditions."

"What would happen if we got there and the bridge was closed?" she persisted.

"We'd be stuck on the mainland until it reopened."

"So we could theoretically be stuck sleeping in the car?"

"We'd get hotel rooms. It's Maine, not Siberia."

But luckily, the clear weather held and the bridge remained open. By the time Alex dropped her off at her car, which Paul had moved to the parking lot as instructed, Holiday felt ready to sleep for twelve hours straight. She'd have to settle for six, but she was confident she could pack some serious REM into that time frame.

"Okay, well . . . I guess this is good night." She stepped out of the truck into the chill wind, looking back at him over her shoulder. "Oh, here, let me give back your coat."

He waved this off. "Keep it. It's freezing."

"Exactly. Aren't you cold?"

He smiled. "I'm a New Englander. This is practically flip-flop weather to me. Speaking of which, can you come over to my place tomorrow?"

She tucked a strand of hair behind her ear, suddenly suffused with self-consciousness. "Sure. Do you want to—"

"I need you to pick an outfit for my big date tomorrow."

"Oh. Yeah, of course. What time?"

He frowned. "You know, now that I think about it, everything I own is five years old and starting to get little holes." He brightened. "I do have a tuxedo, but that's probably overkill."

Holiday laughed. "Alex. Look around you." She threw her arms open to encompass the Wily Whale, the rocky coastline, the shoulder-high snowbanks encircling the plowed parking lot. "Does this look like tuxedo country to you?"

"Only for penguins. But I'm pretty sure this is the wrong pole for them too."

"What you need is nicely fitted premium denim and a pullover."

He furrowed his brow. "That's like pants and a shirt, I'm assuming?"

This time, they both laughed. "Meet me at one. Location TBD. I'll text you."

"Can't wait." He waved and put the truck in reverse. She had to fight the urge to blow him a kiss.

He waited until she had started her car and pulled onto the main road before he left for home. Holiday shivered and turned up the sedan's heaters, which were still blasting cold air. She turned the heat back down and snuggled back into Alex's jacket with way more collar-sniffing than was necessary.

Chapter Fifteen

"MY GOODNESS, YOU look like you're in love!" Michelina, the innkeeper, greeted Holiday with an arched eyebrow and a freshly baked gingersnap.

"I . . . what?" Holiday tried to figure out what gave her away.

"The roses in your cheeks! The sparkle in your eyes. You're positively glowing."

"Oh, I'm just cold," Holiday assured her. "And, you know, salt air is good for the complexion."

"Something here certainly agrees with you." Michelina picked up the paperback mystery on the lobby desk and prepared to resume reading. "Oh, and I have you down for a nine a.m. checkout tomorrow. Does that still fit with your plans?"

Holiday cleared her throat. "Well, if everything goes—"

"I hope it does, because we'll need your room. We're booked solid for Christmas Eve. Lots of out-of-town visitors this year. I guess the secret's out and Alemos is going to be the next Martha's Vineyard."

Holiday tried to chuckle along with Michelina. "Nine a.m. checkout is fine."

"Perfect. Thank you so much for staying with us, dear.

Sleep tight. Oh, and good news—they came and fixed the Wi-Fi today."

"Better late than never." Holiday forced herself to see the silver lining. She still had one more call to make before she collapsed into bed—and at least now she wouldn't have to chat with her sister while shivering out in the snow.

"YOU LIE," NORA accused, her voice soaring upward with indignation. "You're lying to me, you're lying to our parents, but worst of all . . . you're lying to *yourself*."

Holiday sat on the pale-pink duvet and let herself slump back into the softness. "I'm not lying. How dare you?"

"I dare because you've lied every year for the last five years."

"Now that is an exaggeration."

"That's just what a liar would say," Nora shot back.

"Stop with all the name-calling and make sure that my stocking is hung by the chimney with care." Holiday sighed. "I'm not going to disappoint you guys this year. I swear on all that is pink."

"What now?"

"I'm back in the 'Blush and Bashful' boudoir." Holiday knew that her sister would pick up on the *Steel Magnolias* reference, and Nora did not disappoint.

"Pink is mah signature color," Nora drawled.

"I'll be done with my business on Alemos Island by five thirty tomorrow evening. Six at the very latest. I'll be jet-lagged and haggard, but I'll be home as promised."

"What if it keeps snowing?" Nora said.

"It's already snowed for two days. There's no way it can keep snowing. Everything in this world is finite, including precipitation."

"Okay, but what if?"

Holiday sighed again and stared up at the cracks running across the ceiling. "I'll be out of here by six fifteen. And bonus, I now know how to put snow chains on my tires."

Nora paused. "You sure are doing a lot of sighing."

"I'm tired."

"Uh-huh."

"And cold."

"Uh-huh."

"And that's it."

"Again, I must point out that you are a liar," Nora said. "I know something's up."

"Well." Holiday wanted to continue, but she couldn't figure out where to start, where to finish, or anything in between. "It's complicated."

"*Really.*" Nora sounded intrigued. "You usually have an answer for everything. Do you need some sisterly advice?"

"I mean, probably. But it's late, I'm exhausted, and I'd rather break it all down in person over a few chocolate Santas in front of the fireplace in Mom and Dad's living room. Where I will be in approximately twenty-four hours."

"Oh, I can't stay mad at you, you little prevaricator."

"Same to you and more of it."

Excitement crept into Nora's voice. "This is going to be

great. I bought some ironic flannel jammies for you. Just in case."

"You're the best."

"You got that straight. All right, you're on. We're eating candy and spilling tea tomorrow night."

"Believe in miracles," Holiday told her sister. And then she fell asleep, still draped atop the quilt with the phone in her hand and Alex's jacket keeping her warm.

HOLIDAY AWOKE WITH a gasp at the sound of three sharp raps at the door.

"Miss Smith? Dear? Are you in there?"

She scrambled off the bed, blinking in the pale morning sunlight streaming in through the windows. She'd never gotten around to pulling down the shades. Or putting on pajamas. Or showering.

"Yes, I'm here," she croaked, her voice still hoarse from all the hollering she'd done to make herself heard at last night's gala.

"Oh, good." Michelina's laugh sounded a bit forced. "I was starting to worry you'd had a mishap. Slipped in the bathroom, that sort of thing."

Holiday struggled out of the jacket and tried to smooth her hair. "What?"

"It's nine thirty, dear. Checkout time has come and gone."

Holiday winced. She should have been up hours ago,

making calls and arranging dream dates and double-checking Francie's itinerary. "I'm so sorry. I'll be out of here in a second. Just let me take a quick shower and brush my teeth."

She heard rustling and murmuring on the other side of the door. Upon poking her head out into the hallway, she came face-to-face with Michelina, who was dressed in a sparkly green sweater and enough gold jewelry to sink a Spanish galleon.

"We really need the room, dear." Michelina looked disappointed in her wayward guest. "Housekeeping is waiting, and . . ." She trailed off as she took in Holiday's smudged mascara, tousled hair, and sleep-creased cheeks. "On second thought, a few more minutes won't make much difference. Why don't you tidy up a bit and meet me downstairs when you're ready?"

"Thank you." Holiday rubbed her bleary eyes. "Thank you. I'm sorry." Given the innkeeper's expression, she felt compelled to add, "I know how this looks, but I swear I'm not hungover."

Michelina pressed her hand to her chest. "Gracious, dear heart, I don't judge."

"No, of course not, I just . . ." Her shoulders sagged as all the stress and excitement of the last few days swirled up. "I'm trying to do too much in too little time."

"Yuletide malaise." Michelina nodded wisely. "Very common this time of year—especially with women. I'll start a fresh pot of coffee."

Holiday threw her arms around the other woman. "Thank you."

"You take your time getting ready." Michelina readjusted her dangly earrings. "And as for the malaise, I know a fail-safe cure."

Blow off all my obligations and throw myself at the guy I'm supposed to be prepping for a brokenhearted humanitarian? Holiday crossed her fingers.

"A massage at the Alemos Spa." Michelina beamed. "Tell them I sent you and they'll squeeze you in today, I'm sure of it."

"That's so kind of you, but I can't. I have to go arrange for a candlelit cocktail hour at the wine bar and then pick out some men's clothing."

Michelina didn't miss a beat. "Well, try to enjoy yourself. All this rushing around will be done by tomorrow."

"I know." Holiday forced herself to say the next words aloud, reasoning that if she repeated a wish enough times, it would come true. "I'm going to my parents' house tonight. I'll spend Christmas morning with my family."

"Wonderful." Michelina peeked over Holiday's shoulder, presumably to assess the length of time the housekeeping team would need to restore the pink palace to check-in condition. "Luckily, I don't expect the new guest until later today. Her name is Francie, I think. Isn't that lovely? Francie was my grandmother's name."

"I CAN'T BELIEVE the nerve of this hussy." Janine shook her fist as she opened the trunk of Holiday's car so that Holiday could stow her luggage. "First she took your man, now she's taking your hotel room."

Holiday rolled her eyes. "To be fair—"

"Fair, schmair." Janine huffed, blowing little puffs of white into the crisp December air. "She's a poacher of the highest order."

Holiday slammed the trunk closed. "She also took Michelina's grandmother's name, if we're keeping score."

"Figures." Janine pivoted and led the way to her Jeep so that they could drive to the wine bar and start date-planning in earnest.

"But to be fair," Holiday repeated, "I was checking out today anyway. Also, Alex is not my man."

"Only because Fancy Pants McFouffyFace is swooping in after you laid all the groundwork. Doesn't this lady have any shame?"

Holiday had to laugh at Janine's indignation on her behalf. "It wasn't even her idea. Maybe she's just trying to be a good sport and make her grandma happy."

"You're a lot nicer than I am." Janine tugged her woolen beanie over her ears. "If I were in your shoes, I would go all out sabotaging this date. Like old school, no holds barred, *Parent Trap*–style."

"That's the opposite of my job," Holiday pointed out.

"Fine, be that way. Do your job. Follow the rules. But when that poacher smooches Alex under the mistletoe, how are you going to feel?"

Holiday winced at the thought. "Like crap. But my feelings don't matter."

"I beg your pardon?"

"I came to Maine with one goal: to get Alex Sappier under that mistletoe with Fancy Pants McFouffyFace. And you know what? He agreed. That's a minor miracle in and of itself."

"Wrong—it's a *major* miracle."

She straightened her posture. "Alex is willing to uphold his part of the bargain, and I have to uphold mine. That's how wish-granting works."

"But you and Alex have chemistry!" Janine threw up her hands. "You know it, I know it, everybody at the Wily Whale knows it."

"You're just saying that because you want me to move up here and hang out in the library archives with you, tracking down randoms with ill-gotten DNA."

"I mean, obviously. But there's a spark between you two. Don't deny it."

Holiday literally bit her tongue.

"Your face says it all," Janine said. "And PS, you're *wearing his jacket.*"

Holiday started to take off the jacket, got a tiny taste of the windchill on her bare neck, and pulled it back on. "None of this matters." She jumped up and down, trying to shake off all these inconvenient emotions. "I have less than eight hours to plan the most romantic Christmas Eve in all of recorded history. Which is what I was supposed to be doing yesterday and the day before, but instead I've been all over New England swabbing barely legal strangers' cheeks and treasure hunting in attics."

Janine clasped her hands next to her cheek. "The course of true love never did run smooth."

Holiday pivoted one hundred and eighty degrees and headed the other way. "Byeee."

"Oh, come on." Janine caught her elbow. "I'm just giving you a hard time because I'm so completely single. You know I'll help you. But first, coffee."

The mere mention of coffee made Holiday think of Alex. "I don't have time for coffee."

"Make time. You need to eat a good breakfast with a lot of protein to get you through today."

Holiday wrinkled her nose. "Ugh, you sound like my mom."

Janine's smile turned smug. "Would your mom take you to breakfast at a bar?"

"THIS PLACE IS perfect," Holiday admitted as she sipped her caffè Americano and gazed around the wine bar. "It smells great too." She had overlooked the Pine Cone and Tassel during her first few trips down Alemos Island's main street because the building was set back from the sidewalk and surrounded by evergreens and high hedges. The cozy little bistro was housed in a converted log cabin, and the low ceilings, blazing fireplace, and dark wood draped with twinkle lights made for an intimate ambiance.

"Thanks, I make my own candles. This is my seasonal cranberry-fir blend." The owner, a short, wiry redhead sporting a series of tattoos up and down both arms, started swiping at the countertop with a clean dish towel.

"It's lovely." Holiday closed her eyes and inhaled deeply. "Smells like Christmas, but subtle."

"*Bon appetit.*" The bar owner presented Holiday and Janine with two bagel sandwiches laden with egg, cheese, avocado, and tomato. "Would you care for some hot sauce?"

"Always." Janine reached for the bottle of Captain Mowatt's. She offered it to Holiday. "You should try this—it's local."

Holiday was too busy looking around the bar to take a bite. "Do you have a full kitchen in the back?"

"No, just a few toaster ovens. We mostly do appetizers and charcuterie boards, but every once in a while, we'll indulge customers with grilled cheese."

This cottage was so woodsy and crammed with Christmas charm that it would make Martha Stewart writhe with envy. "Are you guys usually busy on Christmas Eve?"

The owner shook her head. "Nope, because I kick everyone out and close up by three p.m."

Holiday nodded as her plan came together. "Is there any chance that I could rent the place out tonight?"

"No can do. I don't work on Christmas Eve night, and I won't ask my staff to, either."

"I completely respect that," Holiday assured her. "I'm not asking for waitstaff or food prep. I just want to rent out the physical space and buy a bottle of your finest champagne."

The owner laughed. "We're not upscale. Our finest

champagne is Blanc de Blanc in a can with a sippy straw."

"Sounds delicious," Janine exclaimed through a mouth full of bagel.

"It does, actually, but I'm setting a very specific scene." Holiday turned all the way around on her spindly wooden bar stool. "It involves fine French bubbly and crystal flutes. Mistletoe and twinkle lights. Cranberry-fir candles and poinsettias."

"Listen, I'll let you rent the space if Janine will vouch for you," the owner relented.

"I vouch," Janine said.

"But you're on your own for the fancy Champagne and crystal flutes. I don't know where you'd find that stuff around here on such short notice."

"Don't say that," Janine warned. "She'll take it as a challenge."

"What about mulled wine?" the owner suggested. "I have a really good recipe using grenache. It smells delicious and tastes even better. Super-Christmassy. It's better when it's been simmering for a few hours, so I could start it this morning and keep it warm all afternoon."

Holiday closed her eyes and pictured it—evergreen boughs amid the rustic wooden rafters, stars sparkling outside the picture window overlooking the snow, glass-walled mugs filled with spiced wine to warm your hands . . .

"What?" Janine demanded.

Holiday's eyes flew open. "Huh?"

"You sighed," Janine informed her. "Are you happy or sad?"

Both. "It's all coming together," Holiday said. "This is going to be so romantic. Like *Northern Exposure* meets *Casablanca.*"

"Hang on—didn't the couple go their separate ways at the end of *Casablanca?*"

"Hmm" was Holiday's only reply.

"Eat your bagel," the owner commanded. Holiday complied and felt better almost immediately in both body and soul.

"Wow, you were right," she said to Janine. "I really needed some protein."

"Told ya."

Holiday pulled out her credit card and prepared to do some serious damage to Mrs. Penewate's petty cash fund. "I need to be in here by three thirty to start decorating. Name your price."

The owner glanced at Janine and threw out an absurdly low rental fee.

Holiday shook her head. "Name a higher price."

"Eh, it's Christmas Eve. Price gouging is grinchy."

"You've created something really special here. You deserve to be compensated for it." Holiday wrote a dollar amount on a napkin and slid it across the bar. "How about that?"

The owner's eyebrows shot up. "What kind of business did you say you were in?"

"I'm a professional wish granter."

The other woman blinked as Holiday handed over her credit card. "I'll say."

"And I promise I won't trash the place."

"Go right ahead. For this amount of money, I can hire a cleanup crew."

"Fantastic! Then it's settled." Holiday folded the napkin on her lap and placed it on the varnished wooden bar top. "I'll be back this afternoon."

"The wine will be mulling," the owner promised. "What are you planning anyway? A marriage proposal?"

"Blind date." Holiday swallowed back the bitter taste in the back of her throat. "For two very deserving people."

"Might as well plan the proposal while you're at it. Between the mulled wine and the mistletoe, these people are done for. They'll probably elope by the end of the night."

Chapter Sixteen

"DON'T LOOK SO glum," Janine urged as they headed back out to the sidewalk. "Alex and Francie are not going to elope. That's absurd."

"Is it, though?" Holiday tugged her mittens on. "They're both single, successful, and attractive. It actually makes perfect sense that they would fall for each other." She paused. "And that's what I should be rooting for. It would be great for my career—I could convince them to do some media puff pieces on how the Christmas concierge delivers true love, along with antique fountain pens and Dandie Dinmont terriers and whatever."

"Is that what you're hoping to get out of this? Media puff pieces?"

"I wouldn't say no."

"The whole time you were telling me about the trip to New Hampshire and the antics in the attic and how you and Alex frosted each other's cookies, you were glowing," Janine said. "Lit up from the inside out."

"That's sweet of you, but I think I'm just sweating from all the stress."

Janine kept going as if Holiday hadn't spoken. "And when you got to the part where he stopped in the middle of a snowstorm to offer assistance to the stranded motorist on the highway . . ." She tipped her face up to the clear morning sunlight. "I honestly thought all the birds in the forest were going to burst into song while a rainbow appeared. And a golden unicorn."

Holiday scrunched up her face. "What exactly is your point?"

"My point is, you yearn and burn for this man."

Holiday did her best to muster some outrage. "You've been sniffing too many cranberry-fir blend candles."

"There's still time to put an end to this madness. Call Alex," Janine urged. "Tell him how you feel."

"No way. That is the dictionary definition of a conflict of interest." Holiday glanced at the time displayed on her phone. "Besides, it's too late. Francie is already on a plane, on her way to meet the boy she pined after from afar."

"Exactly! She's probably stuck on a layover in Detroit and you're right here on Alemos Island. Make your move now while you still have the benefit of geographic proximity."

Holiday allowed herself to consider that possibility for a moment. She set aside the conflicts of interest, the ever-growing to-do list, and her track record of Christmastime heartbreaks and disappointments. She set aside her clients' wishes, her family's wishes, and her own wish to stay emotionally safe and unscathed through another busy season. She allowed herself to imagine calling up Alex—no, showing up at his doorstep—and saying everything she wanted to say to him . . . and *doing* everything she wanted to do to him . . .

There they were—the singing birds, the soaring rainbows, the golden unicorn. She felt herself glowing from the inside out.

And then she shook it off. Because this was real life, and in real life, business agreements needed to be honored and her track record spoke for itself. "No way. I stick to the plan."

"Says the lady who's still snuggled up in his jacket."

Holiday threw up her hands. "I don't have any choice in the matter—he still has my coat in his car. This is just a matter of practicality, so I don't freeze to death."

Janine stopped walking and looked at her.

"It's not like I'm wearing his class ring at the Friday night football game," Holiday sputtered.

Janine tilted her head, considering. "Actually, it kind of is."

"And I'm not going to double-cross my client and her granddaughter, who is braving Christmas Eve air travel, for my own selfish whims." Holiday stopped in the middle of the sidewalk and crossed her arms. "This blind date is happening, and everyone is going to have an enchanted evening in a winter wonderland, and that's that."

"Are you trying to convince me or yourself?"

"I don't have to convince anyone of anything. What I have to do is meet Alex—aka, the target, the mark, the *commodity*—and make sure he is appropriately attired to be the North Woods version of Prince Charming. So I am asking you, kindly and respectfully, to stop needling me and help me figure out where I can find some decent men's clothing by one o'clock this afternoon."

"Spinone's," Janine said without a moment's hesitation. "It's a block down from the library. Super-touristy and super-spendy, but they have good stuff, and since Alex is paying, price is no object."

"Thank you." Holiday noted this information in her phone.

"And tell you what—after you introduce Prince Charming to the princess, why don't you come over to my house and we'll open a bottle of prosecco and eat Christmas cookies until we burst?"

"That sounds amazing, but we'll have to plan a raincheck. I'm going home tonight, and nothing's going to stop me."

Janine didn't say anything, but she didn't have to—her face was doing all the talking.

"What?" Holiday demanded.

"Nothing. But, um, have you looked at the weather forecast?"

"So it's going to snow. Again. So what?"

"'Nor'easter' is actually the term they are using."

"No problem. I can put on snow chains now." Holiday attempted to pat herself on the back. "I'm unstoppable."

Janine nodded and didn't argue, which just made Holiday protest more.

"This is the year I'm keeping my promises to everyone. Including my family. Including myself. I am going to be home for Christmas morning come hell or high water or Nor'easters. As God is my witness." She shook her mittened fist. "Besides, look how sunny it is. Maybe the forecast is wrong. Not a cloud in the sky."

THE FIRST SNOWFLAKE fell as Holiday approached the door to Spinone's Clothiers. She glanced at the tiny white ice crystal resting on her coat sleeve, glanced up at the clouds gathering on the horizon, and sternly instructed the weather to "Cease and desist." Then she bustled inside the shop, which, just as Janine had promised, was a veritable bastion of bougie—stacks of cashmere sweaters, waxed canvas barn coats, and shearling-lined boots that cost more than Italian designer stilettos. A line of well-heeled city folk was queued up at the cash register, and the Yeah Yeah Yeahs' version of "All I Want for Christmas" blasted from the speaker system.

She checked the time: 1:03. Three minutes behind schedule. Upon dialing Alex's number, a cell phone started ringing behind the burlap curtain of a nearby dressing room.

"Alex?" she called. "Is that you?"

"I'm way ahead of you." His voice drifted over the curtain. "Already trying on my third shirt." At the sound of his voice, all the tingles—emotional *and* physical—from last night flooded through her. She was a bit shocked at the intensity of her response.

But that was the thing about good chemistry—it was powerful. It was immediate. It was nothing more than hormones roiling around together. She could counteract chemistry.

And there it was—her new mantra. She'd repeat it until she actually believed it.

As if on cue, Paul strode over, carrying a stack of sweaters and sport coats. His face lit up when he saw Holiday. "You're finally here. I'm a man of many talents, but personal stylist ain't one of them." He shoved the pile of clothes toward her.

She opened her arms to accept all the merino and tweed. "Hi, Paul, good to see you too."

"Guess my work here is done." Paul didn't try to hide his relief. "See you later."

"Hey!" Alex stepped out from the dressing room. The cascade of tingling started anew. "You don't get to escape so easily."

"But she's here." Paul pointed at Holiday. "And I'm hungry."

"You helped break Mom's glass star, you can help shop for clothes."

"Shopping for clothes is almost worse than telling Mom about the star. Almost." Paul produced his cell phone and nodded at Holiday. "I'm ordering a sandwich. You want anything?"

"A strawberry milkshake would be great," she replied. *I can counteract chemistry, I can counteract chemistry, I can—*

"What about me?" Alex demanded.

"You get what you get." Paul stepped outside the shop to complete his food order.

"Not bad." Holiday gave Alex an exaggerated once-over. He was clad in navy pants and a black-and-green watch plaid shirt. "Except the navy and the black don't one hundred percent go together."

"Try telling Paul that." Alex stepped back to give her a once-over of his own. "Nice jacket."

"Yeah, sorry, I forgot to give it back last night." Holiday forced herself to take off the warm wool jacket and hand it to him.

"You can keep it," he offered. "Looks good on you."

"No, I couldn't possibly. You've already done so much for me." She smiled, thinking of yesterday's adventures.

"If you're giving this back, then I'm buying you a new coat while we're here." He cut off her attempts to protest. "The one you left in my truck is still damp and covered in road salt. You'll need something to keep you warm during the snowstorm."

"It's not snowing," Holiday insisted.

He glanced over her shoulder and out the plate glass storefront window.

"Not a word," she warned.

"Can I help you?" a perky, ponytailed sales associate interrupted.

"Absolutely. Thank you so much for asking." Holiday glanced around the store displays and made some swift executive decisions. "This gentleman would like to try on a gray V-necked sweater, please. Maybe a gray cable crewneck as well."

"It will bring out your eyes." The saleslady sidled up to Alex and started brushing off his shoulders and picking imaginary lint from the front of his sweater. "Wool or a silk-cotton blend for the crewneck?"

Holiday recited her manta about counteracting chemistry and threw in a few lines from the Serenity Prayer in her effort to remain unaffected in the face of this flirtation. "Both, if you have them."

"Hang on; how many things do I have to try on?" Alex demanded.

"Enough to find the perfect fit." Holiday settled into a rustic wooden chair next to the dressing rooms. "The sooner you get started, the sooner we'll be finished."

Alex caught the associate's eye before she turned away. "And the lady would like to see something in a puffy down parka, please."

The associate seemed momentarily disappointed that he hadn't responded to her advances, but the prospect of increased commission revived her spirits. "I'm on it. We got a shipment of cherry-red Monclers yesterday. I'll go in the back and find them."

"Sounds great. Thanks for your help." He looked at Holiday. "If I'm trying stuff on, you're trying stuff on."

"I'll try stuff on, but I'm not getting a cherry-red Moncler," she informed him. To the sales associate, she explained, "I tend to stick to neutral colors in winter."

"Let me see what I can do." The associate bustled back into the crowd.

"Try something new," Alex advised her. "Live a little. Get outside your comfort zone."

"I'm in Alemos Island, Maine. That's so far out of my comfort zone, I needed GPS and a lesson in snow chain application."

"It's good to try new things." He caught her gaze and held it. "Keeps life exciting."

"Spoken like a man who's discovered the thrill of wearing elf shoes at a black-tie gala." She tried to keep her tone light. "But cheap thrills are one thing. Do you know how much Moncler coats cost? They're like the Ferrari of outerwear."

He shrugged. "My treat."

"Alex. I can't accept extravagant gifts from you." She felt so awkward, she had to turn away from him. "We're not . . . I mean, we can't . . ."

"Don't overthink it," he advised her. "Sometimes a coat is just a coat."

The sales associate returned just as the ensuing silence became truly uncomfortable. "Here you go. I took a guess at the sizes." She handed a trio of gray sweaters to Alex. "And for you . . ." She gave Holiday a knee-length maroon parka to try on. "We have one of these left. I thought we'd sold out, but someone reshelved it in the wrong section. If cherry red isn't your thing, I thought you might prefer something less flashy."

The jacket was beautiful, the exact shade of a dark-red poinsettia. Holiday put it on, zipped it up, and immediately felt twenty degrees warmer. Also, she couldn't stop admiring herself in the full-length mirror between the dressing rooms.

"Fab," the sales associate proclaimed.

"You don't think it's too—I don't know—Rudolph's nose, do you?" Holiday knew, even as she said it, what the answer would be. Maybe that's why she'd said it.

"You look beautiful," Alex said, frozen halfway into pulling a sweater over his white T-shirt.

The sales associate beamed. "You heard the man."

"All right, you talked me into it." Holiday took the coat off and started hunting for a price tag around the inside of the collar.

"Nope." Alex plucked the garment out of her hands and gave it back to the sales associate. "My treat. And no need for a bag. She'll wear it out of the store."

"Thank you." Holiday couldn't quite make eye contact with him, so she gazed at the wood-paneled wall behind them.

The saleswoman, scenting last-minute desperation and the potential for even more commission, circled back around. "We have a pair of garnet-and-yellow gold earrings that would go perfectly with this." She glanced at Alex. "If you want, I could ring them up—"

"No, thank you," Holiday said firmly. "That will be all for me." She put her hands on Alex's shoulders and steered him back into the dressing room. "Stop worrying about my wardrobe and start worrying about your own."

"Okay, lunch'll be ready in ten, so pick something and let's get out of here." Paul rejoined them with a spring in his step. "Alex, I took pity on you and ordered that sandwich with the peppers you like."

"Hang on, we've got a few more sweaters to see," Holiday told him.

Paul smiled as though he were about to pat her on the

head. "It doesn't matter. They all look the same."

"They do not!" Holiday turned to the saleslady for back-up. "The different textures are night and day, not to mention the difference in navy versus gray with his skin tone."

Alex's phone pinged on the other side of the burlap curtain. "Give me a second, guys—I've got to take this."

After a few moments of barely audible murmuring, Alex cleared his throat. "Hey, Paul, could you come in here for a second? Mom wants to talk to both of us."

Paul's eyes widened and he cast a panicked glance at Holiday. "About what?"

"Why don't you come find out?" A hint of impatience crept into Alex's voice.

Holiday wandered around the store for a bit, trying to afford the brothers some privacy. After debating and rejecting the idea of quilted, down-filled "après-ski joggers," she returned to the dressing room area, just in time to hear Paul say, "I'll be there at seven, Mom. Does that work for you?" After a few seconds of silence, Alex said, "I understand it's Christmas Eve, but I have a prior commitment . . . No, I can't tell you what it is, but Paul will be there at seven, and I'll be there as soon as I can. I'm sorry, but that's the best I can do. Hang on, I have a work call on the other line." His voice sounded strained with frustration.

Holiday did another lap around the store and returned to a heated brotherly debate so loud it was impossible not to overhear.

"Why is this happening now?" Paul asked. "Do they not understand it's Christmas Eve?"

"No one in biotech cares about taking time off for the holidays," Alex replied. "Yet another reason why I left."

"Just tell them they'll have to wait," Paul urged.

"If this deal falls apart, half of my team might lose their jobs," Alex said.

"They're not your team anymore," Paul replied. "If the new CEO sucks, that's on him."

"I'm not going to cut them all loose like that," Alex said. "It's not their fault he sucks."

"What's the latest you can schedule a Zoom call tonight?" Paul asked.

"Whenever I'm done with this blind date." Alex sounded beyond frustrated. "So I don't know . . . eight? Eight thirty?"

"But you already told Mom you were coming over."

"You know what?" Alex's tone had gone from strained and stressed to clipped and cold. "Everyone is going to have to deal with disappointment. I'm doing everything I can here."

Holiday cleared her throat loudly on the other side of the dressing room curtain. No one responded.

"You can't be in three places at once," Paul said. "Work is important, family is important . . . Maybe you could reschedule the date?"

Holiday stilled and listened with all her might.

"No, I have to do it." Alex sounded angry for the first time since Holiday had met him. "I made a deal, and I have to do my part." There was another pause. "I can't believe I got myself into this."

"It'll be over soon," Paul said. "By tomorrow morning,

this will all be over."

"Twelve hours and counting." There was an odd ripping noise on the other side of the burlap curtain. "In the meantime, I have to try on two more sweaters to earn my freedom, so if you'll excuse me . . ."

Holiday recoiled at the bitterness in his voice. Of course, she realized that Alex had gone out of his way and rearranged his schedule for the last three days on her behalf . . . but she had done the same. And no matter how chaotic the situation had gotten, she'd enjoyed their time together. She'd thought he had as well.

Paul exited the dressing room and avoided eye contact with Holiday, who had moved herself safely out of earshot to the shoe section. Five minutes later, Alex strode out carrying a stack of pants and sweaters. "Any of these'll work." He placed the folded garments on the chair next to Holiday and handed his credit card to Paul. "Thanks."

He turned to Holiday without a hint of a smile. "See you at five."

"Listen, I'm a wish granter, not a warden." She lifted her chin. "If you need to bail, go ahead and bail. We can make the date work for next week or whatever."

She heard the ripping noise again. When she glanced down, she saw that he was systematically shredding an old paper receipt. "I'll be at the Pine Cone and Tassel at five sharp," he told her.

"It's not worth it to make you eat brie and drink wine on demand if it's going to cost a bunch of people their jobs," she said.

He furrowed his brow. "How much did you hear?"

"Enough." She squared her shoulders. "And I get it. There's a lot of pressure this time of year. Lots of obligations and choices and what basically boils down to emotional blackmail."

Paul whispered, "Mom," and nodded.

"I'm no blackmailer." She stared him right in the eye. "I don't want you doing me any favors or resenting me because I forced your hand. If you bail, I won't be disappointed. This isn't personal."

The ripping turned into crunching as he crumpled the receipt into a tiny ball. "Nothing's personal with you. You've made that clear."

She folded her arms and told herself that she had no idea what he was talking about. "I have a job and I'm doing it. With or without you."

"I don't see how . . ." Paul started. He trailed off when they both turned to him, scowling. "I'll go get in line."

Holiday turned back to Alex, her exasperation growing by the second. "I'm letting you off the hook. I'm not disappointed. I'm not resentful. Why are you mad?"

"You're never disappointed," he shot back. "You're too busy getting out of the way before anything disappointing can happen."

She snatched up a cashmere cardigan and held it to her chest. "What does that even mean?"

He waited until she met his gaze and held it. "It means that you've found someone who wants to make your wishes come true and you won't let me."

She was so stunned, all she could manage to say in reply was "That's not true." Because she feared it wasn't true. Other men had said the same, and it hadn't been true. But oh, how she *wanted* it to be true. The depth of her longing was terrifying.

"I know it's true from my side," he said.

She clutched the cashmere, feeling as though she was right on the edge of falling. But with a deep breath, she pulled herself back from the brink. She had just met this man. Even if he meant it when he said he wanted to make her wishes come true, she wasn't sure she could do the same for him. What was the point of squandering her career and other people's hopes and dreams if, in the end, she couldn't give him what he wanted?

She lowered her voice, and her whole body slumped. "I have promises to keep."

There ensued a long pause, during which she couldn't bring herself to look at him.

"Pick a sweater and I'll wear it and that's the end of that. See you at five." He strode out of the store without a backward glance.

Chapter Seventeen

HOLIDAY HURRIED OUT of the shop, only to hear footsteps pounding on the sidewalk behind her. She whirled around to find herself face-to-face with Paul. He was holding a pair of shopping bags, from which he pulled the puffy maroon jacket.

"You forgot your coat," he said.

She opened her mouth to protest, but he interrupted. "I already paid for it, and I am not about to stand in that line again to return it. Do me a favor and don't argue."

"Thank you." Holiday slipped into the luxurious jacket and tugged up the zipper. Despite all the down insulation and windproof fabric, she felt cold from the inside out. "I guess I've done enough arguing for today."

Paul lifted the remaining shopping bag. "At least Alex'll be well dressed. I wasn't sure if he'd decided on anything, so I bought 'em all. If there's something he doesn't want, let *him* stand in the return line."

Holiday shivered as the snowflakes started to accumulate on her hair. "I'm so sorry you had to see that."

Paul laughed. "Ooh, a thirty-second verbal spat. I'm scarred for life."

His goofiness was infectious, and she almost smiled too.

"I'm serious. That wasn't very professional of me."

"Who cares?" He scoffed. "You and Alex passed the 'professional' stage of things a country mile ago."

Holiday stepped to the far edge of the sidewalk as a family with a dog and a stroller bustled by. She jammed her hands in her pockets and tried to scrape together the last vestiges of her unflappable business persona. "I'm not sure I know what you mean."

Paul laughed again. "Save it. I already heard about the elf uniforms." He shook his head at the mental image. "Listen, I know Alex said some rough stuff back there—"

"Nothing as rough as what I said," Holiday interjected.

"Don't be so hard on yourself. You just got caught in the Christmas crossfire." Paul seemed unaware of the snowflakes pelting his face. "My mom is harassing him, work is harassing him—"

"And I am harassing him."

"Nah, you're helping him. He should be grateful." Paul stepped closer to her and confided, "It was probably the sweaters that set him off. He's been prickly about sweaters ever since that incident with Kathryn."

It took Holiday a moment to place the name. "The ex-girlfriend?"

Paul's eyebrows shot up. "He told you about Kathryn? You guys are definitely past the professional stage."

"Maybe a little bit," Holiday allowed. "He mentioned that she rearranged his kitchen."

"You don't know the half of it." Paul's tone suggested that he had been holding in these grievances for months.

"That woman was a control freak like none other. She tried to act all easy-breezy in the beginning, but I am here to tell you that was a ruse. She was a total type A, and the A stood for . . ." He held up his index finger. "Um . . . authoritative? No, *authoritarian*. That's right, right?"

"Exactly right." Holiday nodded. "Alex told me about the preemptive engagement ring photos."

"Did he tell you about how she tried to overhaul his diet? And his wardrobe?" Paul was on a roll.

"What was wrong with his diet and his wardrobe?" Holiday was so intrigued by all this, she forgot to be cold.

"Nothing! But it wasn't the way she wanted him to eat and dress. Did he tell you they broke up over a sweater?"

"No."

"Yeah. At Christmas, actually." Paul spread out his hands, inviting her to imagine the scene. "They were going to have dinner at a fancy restaurant with her family and my mom, and so Alex put on a sweater my mom had given him."

"That's sweet."

"That's not what Kathryn said. She wanted to him to wear a different color or pattern or whatever, and he held his ground, and they broke up right there in his closet." Paul crossed his arms and nodded. "The sweater drama was *intense*."

Holiday winced as she remembered the way she'd shoved sweaters and issued orders at Alex in the dressing room. "Well, if I'd known that, I wouldn't have pushed the sweater agenda today."

"You couldn't have known." Paul gave her a pat on the back. "And I'm no psychologist, but I'd say it wasn't really about the sweater."

"Neither was today." She sighed.

"And listen, it's not like that guy doesn't know how to work under pressure. He lived that start-up life for ten years." Paul's laugh turned dry. "I don't feel sorry for him. He already has a nonprofessional thing going with you, *plus* he gets to go on a date with the hot girl from high school who he doesn't even remember! And meanwhile, I'm going to our mom's house tonight, and she'll be twiddling her thumbs the whole time, waiting for Alex to show up." He shook his head at Holiday. "Life, man."

"Life," she echoed. "Hey, you want to come decorate the wine bar for Alex's date tonight?"

"I sure don't."

She gave him a jaunty wave. "Well, then, *adieu*, and a merry Christmas to you."

He responded with a salute. "*Feliz Navidad*, baby."

"OOF." HOLIDAY CARRIED in the last pair of potted poinsettias and hoisted them up on the back wall of the bar along with the dozen other flowers she'd already hauled in. The addition of pine garlands and votive candles set the scene for intimacy and indulgence.

I can't believe I got myself into this.

She couldn't stop thinking about Alex's words—or his

tone—as she decked the bar with boughs of holly. The look on his face when he'd said nothing was ever personal with her. If she could go back and do things differently . . .

But there was no going back. She wasn't going to let herself spiral into doubt and despair. Not right now. She had a job to do, and she was going to do get it done, then retreat to the loving family Christmas she'd missed for too many years. She could practically smell her mother's cinnamon rolls. Or was that the mulled wine starting to scald?

Holiday rushed into the kitchen area to stir the wine and turn down the heat on the stovetop. She'd put a wheel of brie to warm in the countertop oven and arranged a variety of nuts, crackers, and dried fruits on a marble cutting board. Now, she had only to select the perfect background music and wait for her guests to arrive. Francie had texted from the airport in Portland to notify Holiday that she'd arrived but was "anticipating possible road delays due to the weather." Even without glancing out the windows, Holiday could hear the blizzard gathering strength as tiny particles of ice pelted the glass.

I can't believe I got myself into this.

She couldn't do anything about the weather or Alex's history of intense sweater drama or her own rocky romantic past, but she could ensure that she'd done everything in her power to provide Francie with the date she—and her grandmother—had been dreaming of for the last twenty years. She'd created the perfect playlist full of soothing Christmas ballads by the likes of Andrea Bocelli and Norah Jones, then fastened a tiny sprig of mistletoe above the bar. She figured that, no matter how much snow came down, she'd be able to make it off the island as long as she said her goodbyes by six. Janine had offered to lock up and return the keys to the bar's owner.

And, speaking of Janine, a text binged in: *There's some chatter about closing the bridge because of the snow. Any chance you can get the rendezvous started early?*

Holiday grimaced as she replied: *Not unless we can move the whole thing to Portland right now. I only need a few more hours.*

Janine texted back the "fingers crossed" emoji.

Holiday helped herself to a tiny sip of mulled wine—just to make sure it still tasted delicious—and comforted herself with the thought that in mere hours, she'd be under her parents' roof. She would be warm and well-fed. She could take a break from red-eye flights and scratchy hotel sheets and the frantic stress of December. And Alex. And whatever was or wasn't happening between them.

If only the bridge would stay open for a few more hours.

Chapter Eighteen

THE TINY BELL atop the bar's front door tinkled at 5:03 p.m. Holiday wiped her hands on a dish towel, tucked her hair behind her ear, and stepped out from the kitchen area holding the charcuterie board in both hands.

"Welcome to Alemos Island." She placed the charcuterie board on the bar and inwardly died as she beheld the woman who she couldn't stop thinking of as her competition.

"Hello, I'm Francie Penewate." The tall, willowy brunette with rosy cheeks and a porcelain complexion looked like a former model who had given up the runways of Milan to claim her true birthright as European aristocracy. Her hair was glossy, her teeth were perfect, even her scarf was tied in the sort of elegant Parisian knot that Holiday had never been able to master. "You must be Holiday Smith. My grandmother told me all about you." The model-slash-marchioness took off her leather gloves and offered a handshake. "Thank you for arranging all of this—it looks as though you've gone to a lot of trouble."

"It's my pleasure," Holiday assured her. "Thanks for braving all the Christmas Eve airport insanity to get here."

"I wouldn't have missed it," Francie said. "I adore travel, but I've never been to Maine. Can you believe that? I've been to Zanzibar, Antarctica, and Easter Island, but not Maine."

"I heard you're staying at the Alemos Inn tonight," Holiday said, opting to leave out the part where Francie would be taking over her vacated room. "Enjoy the breakfast scones. They're transformative."

"I'll make a note of that." Francie took off her navy overcoat, revealing an almost painfully thin frame. "My grandmother made me promise to eat well on this trip. I've lost fifteen pounds since my divorce. I call it the Despondency Diet."

Holiday slid the charcuterie board toward her. "You know what helps with that? Three different kinds of cheese."

"You're very kind." Francie glanced back at the door. "When is Alex supposed to arrive?"

"Um . . ." *Five minutes ago.* "Any time now. The roads are kind of a mess."

"So I noticed." Francie loaded up a cracker with brie and cranberry preserves. "I was lucky enough to find a snowplow to follow all the way into town."

And she hadn't dropped her belongings to be run over by said snow plow. *Of course.*

"No issues with the bridge?" Holiday pressed.

Francie shook her head. She took a few minutes to commune with the cheese. "I wonder what he'll be like."

"Alex?" *The guy who's now ten minutes late?*

"Mm-hmm." Francie's smile was self-deprecating. "I'm sure my grandmother divulged every detail. I had such a crush on him all through high school. He was tall and good-looking, so smart, so quick . . . but he was kind too. Never mean at someone else's expense." She fluffed up her perfect hair. "I hope that success in the tech world hasn't rotted his soul."

"It hasn't," Holiday blurted out.

"He never even looked my way," Francie went on. "And I was so shy, I barely looked at him. I just nurtured a ridiculous crush for years and never said a word. I guess I was waiting for a bolt of lightning to come out of the sky and make him see that I was the perfect match for him."

"High school." Holiday shook her head. "Good times."

"My awkward stage lasted longer than it had any right to." Francie laughed. "It was excruciating. And then Alex stayed in Massachusetts for college, I went off to the west coast, and we never saw each other again." She took a big bite of cheese and crackers before confessing, "Which is not to say that I didn't look him up now and then on social media over the years."

"Isn't that the whole purpose of social media?" Holiday sympathized.

Francie sighed and sank onto a bar stool. "I suppose this whole thing seems pathetic to you."

"Not at all." Holiday sat down next to her. "There are some guys who just get to you. Especially guys like him."

Francie laughed. "You know the feeling?"

"Well, no, I mean, not with *him*, obviously." Holiday was speaking too quickly, but she couldn't seem to slow down. "But I think almost everyone has someone from the past they think about. The one who got away."

"I should have married a guy like Alex." Francie rested

her chin on her hand. Her gold watch gleamed in the candlelight. "Maybe next time."

Holiday cursed herself for creating such a cozy, inviting tableau. The bar owner was right—her targets were going to fall in love and live happily ever after. *Why* must she be so good at her job?

"That's the spirit," she said to Francie. "The best is yet to come."

"Definitely. I've learned my lesson. Next time, I'm picking a completely different type of guy and having a completely different type of wedding." Francie looked around. "Might I trouble you for a drink?"

Holiday hopped off the stool and hastened to provide a glass cup full of mulled wine. "Cheers."

"Thank you." Francie inhaled the scent of cinnamon and oranges before taking a sip. "Delicious. Anyway, as I was saying, next go-round, there'll be none of that *Town & Country* fuss and frill. Next time, I'll say my vows to Elvis at the drive-through chapel in Vegas."

Holiday narrowed her eyes. "Are you sure? You seem a bit too . . ."

"Straitlaced?" Francie laughed. "Well, that's how my mother and grandmother brought me up. But now that I'm starting over, I'm ready to do things my way. I wonder if Alex is a drive-through chapel type of man."

Finally—*finally*—Alex walked through the door and took off his coat to reveal the gray sweater that really did set off his eyes.

"Sorry I'm late." He shot Holiday a furtive glance. "I had

to deal with a work emergency."

"Hello again. I'm Francie Penewate." Francie got to her feet with the grace of a prima ballerina and offered her hand to him. "Thank you so much for humoring my grandmother. You're a very good sport."

"Oh, it was all her doing." He pointed to Holiday. "I mean, it's my pleasure."

"Well, since we're going to spend all night getting to know each other, I'll ask the first question," Francie said. "Alex, do you enjoy going to Vegas?"

"Yes?" It came out as more of a question than a reply. "I'm not much of a gambler, but I'll fly out there for a weekend every few years."

"Fair enough." Francie sat back down and indicated that Alex should take the stool next to hers. "Now it's your turn. Ask me anything."

He walked toward the bar, but stopped in front of Holiday instead of Francie. "Can I talk to you for one second?"

Holiday paused with one hand hovering over the charcuterie board. "Um . . ."

Alex turned on a heart-melting smile as he apologized to Francie. "It's business-related. I'll be right back and then I want to hear all about you."

"Go for it." Francie turned her attention back to the charcuterie. "I've got wine and cheese. That's all I need to keep me happy."

"I like your style," Alex told her. Then he addressed Holiday in a low murmur. "I'll keep it short, I promise."

She led the way into the kitchen area, turned her back on

him, and busied herself with stirring the mulled wine. "Whatever this is about, it can wait, Alex."

"No, it can't."

Something in his tone made her turn around.

"Are you still planning to leave the island tonight and go home?"

She had so much she wanted to say, so much she wanted to ask. But she had made a commitment, and she was out of time. "Yes," she said into the giant steel pot simmering on the stove.

He let out a long, slow breath. "Okay. Then there's something you need to know."

She turned around and met his gaze. "I'm serious. We cannot get into this right now."

He set his jaw. "It's thirty-three degrees outside."

Her wary gaze turned into a bemused stare. "What?"

"It's thirty-three degrees, which means that all that snow coming down is turning into sleet. The roads are going to be incredibly slick—especially on the bridge."

Holiday recalled the wording of the sign by the overpass to the island. "Bridge freezes before road."

He nodded. "If you're planning to leave tonight, you need to get on the road right now."

Her jaw dropped. "Are you kicking me out?"

"I'm trying to make sure you get what you want," he countered.

There were so many things she wanted to say in response, none of them helpful or appropriate for this time and place.

He was still looking at her intently. "Thirty-three degrees," he repeated.

Nothing about their time together, nothing about seeing each other again, not even a goodbye. Holiday took off her apron and accepted that "thirty-three degrees" was all that Alex was going to offer her right now. He was trying to give her what she wanted. She had set the terms that none of this was personal.

"Thank you," she told him. She let herself look at him for a long, lingering moment before heading back into the main room.

"Francie, you're all set for your accommodations tonight, is that correct?" she asked.

Francie beamed. "Yes, ma'am."

"Then I'm going to make myself scarce and let you two get to know each other. Here's my number. Text if you need anything." She started to scribble on a paper napkin.

"I have your number," Francie assured her.

"I'll make sure she gets back to the inn safe and sound," Alex promised.

Francie's beam brightened. "My knight in shining snow tires."

"My friend Janine lives just down the street. I'm going to text her right now and ask her to come hang out in the kitchen until you guys are done." Holiday scribbled another number down on the napkin.

Francie laughed. "We don't need a chaperone."

"Someone needs to stir the wine and lock the place up when you're done."

"Hey." Alex touched her wrist. "Go. I got this."

Holiday hurried into the backroom, pulled on her parka, and wound her scarf around her neck in a distinctly non-Parisian manner. She strode out the exit to the tiny parking lot behind the bistro, where the wind was sweeping the snow up into icy dervishes that stung her cheeks and eyes. Despite the meteorological theatrics, the wind wasn't that frigid.

Alex was right. The temperature hovered right around thirty-three degrees—ideal conditions for black ice and treacherous driving. But a few days in rural Maine had been sufficient to vanquish her residual snow-related trauma. Holiday knew she could handle thirty-three degrees. She could handle anything.

The wine bar's metal door slammed shut behind her, cutting off the warm golden light and the smell of spices and the sound of soft male and female laughter. Holiday tapped the key fob to unlock her car and sternly informed herself that there was no good reason for the pang of loneliness in her heart. She was finally, *finally,* going to have a Christmas morning with her family. She had a full tank of gas and a steady stream of travel podcasts to get her through the drive. Alex and Francie were having a grand old time, and there didn't seem to be any awkwardness between them at all. Everyone's wishes had come true.

"Bah humbug," she muttered as she climbed into her car and fastened her seat belt.

She forced herself to switch from Scrooge-isms to Christmas carols as she turned onto the main road and headed toward the edge of town. Nothing like an *a cappella* version of "Jingle Bells" at the top of your lungs to really get the spirit.

She ramped up the vocal dramatics as she approached the bridge. "Oh, what fun it is to ride in a one-horse open sleigh . . . *crap!*" She slammed on the brakes, sending the car slip-sliding to a stop as she saw the flashing yellow lights. A portable, illuminated sign announced: BRIDGE CLOSED TO TRAFFIC.

Chapter Nineteen

HOLIDAY GRIPPED THE steering wheel with both hands and let out a scream worthy of *The Exorcist*. When she was out of breath, she bowed her head, touched her brow to the steering wheel, gathered her strength, and screamed again.

Behind her, headlights approached, then faded away as the other car turned around and headed back toward town.

After allowing herself a few more minutes of existential freak-out, Holiday gathered up the tattered remnants of her dignity and admitted defeat. She drove back to the Pine Cone and Tassel at five miles per hour, her tires crunching against the layers of ice on the road. She hoped Janine had already arrived to serve as chaperone. She also hoped that Janine had an extra bed or a sofa to crash on, or she'd be sleeping in her car tonight. Thank goodness she'd just procured the warmest down jacket in all the land.

And now it was time for her least favorite Christmas tradition: She was going to have to call her sister and her parents and notify them that she'd flaked on them at the last possible moment. Again.

Janine's car wasn't in the bistro's parking lot. Holiday assumed that meant that the side streets were impassable or that her new friend was consumed with her own seasonal drama to the point that she couldn't deal with anyone else's right now. Fair enough.

Holiday slogged her way through a knee-high snow drift and reentered the bar. Francie and Alex, seated at the bar and communing over the charcuterie plate, both straightened up, surprised.

"You're back?" Francie said. "What happened?"

"They closed the bridge," Alex predicted.

Holiday nodded. "I'm here for the night. If you need anything, I'll be in the kitchen." *Sobbing and swearing in my mind.* "Otherwise, keep enjoying yourselves and try to forget that I'm here."

Francie slid off her barstool. "About that . . . may I have a quick word with you?"

Holiday glanced at Alex, whose expression was impassive. "Um, sure, come on back."

Francie ducked around the corner and beckoned Holiday into the drafty alcove by the stovetop. "Listen, this has been lovely, and I truly appreciate all your efforts, but I think I'm going to call it a night."

"Already?"

Francie nodded, wrinkling her nose a bit.

Holiday glanced at the clock above the sink. "But you've only been on your date for twenty-seven minutes!"

"I know, I know. I'm impossible." Francie's eyes widened as a thought occurred. "Please don't tell my grandmother."

"I would never."

"I know she's paying for all this, and I so appreciate the

thought."

"She paid me to set up the date," Holiday clarified. "There's no mandatory time minimum. Everyone's contractual obligations are now fulfilled."

"You're the best." Francie grabbed a glass mug from the shelf and ladled up another cup of mulled wine. "Here's to the only upside of being caught on an island in the middle of a blizzard—I'll obviously be walking back to the inn, so might as well drink up, eh?"

"'Tis the season."

"Come on." Francie grabbed a second mug. "Have a drink with me."

"I shouldn't," Holiday protested. "You're technically my client."

"Not anymore. I just fired you."

Those words had never sounded so sweet. "You've got a point there."

"Excellent." Francie dipped the ladle back into the pot.

"If you don't mind my asking, though . . . what happened?" Holiday had to know. "Why are you cutting this short?"

"Look. Alex seems great." Francie took a big gulp of wine. "He's charming, he's witty, et cetera, et cetera. And, I mean, can that man fill out a cashmere sweater or what?"

They both laughed.

"He's exactly what I wanted the whole time I was growing up." Francie nibbled her lower lip. "But now that I've finally grown up, I guess I don't want that anymore."

Holiday took a seat on the stool next to the stove and

listened.

"My mother and my grandmother brought me up to be a lady. Sit up straight, use the proper fork, cross your legs at the ankle rather than the knees." Francie boosted herself up to sit on the chipped laminate countertop. "I myself find it all to be a little extra."

Holiday felt compelled to say, "I don't think Alex has any expectations about fork usage or leg crossing." Before she could stop herself, she added, "He gave me a piggyback through a blizzard last night because I gave my elf shoes to a preschooler."

Francie was so caught up in her own conflicts that she didn't even respond to this. "Alex isn't the issue. I am. I'm ready to conclude the pearl-wearing, ankle-crossing chapter of my life. I've already married and divorced one sweater-wearing Ivy League millionaire. I don't need another."

Holiday had to chuckle. "You've married one sweater-wearing, Ivy League millionaire, you've married 'em all."

Francie had the decency to blush at this. "I know how ridiculous this sounds. How spoiled and entitled."

"Holiday?" Alex's voice drifted in from the barroom. "You guys okay back there?"

"Yeah, we're just having some wine," she called back. "Apparently, the party has moved to the kitchen."

Francie continued her reverie, undeterred. "But this time around, I'm looking for someone rougher around the edges. Someone rugged and adventurous." She closed her eyes, no doubt conjuring up her vision of the perfect man. "I don't want someone who can fly me around the world first-class, I want someone who can *teach* me how to fly."

"You want flying lessons?" Alex appeared in the doorway.

Francie's eyes flew open, and she regarded him with renewed interest. "Yes, one thousand times, yes. Don't tell me you're a flight instructor on top of all your other accomplishments?"

"I am not." Alex scrolled through his phone. "But I know a guy." He showed her a photo of Paul in the seaplane.

"Well, *hello*." Francie seized the phone and scrutinized the picture. "He looks kind of familiar."

"He's my brother," Alex said. "He went to high school with us too."

"Really? How did I not notice him?" Francie zoomed in to get a better look at Paul's face. "He's handsome. But not too handsome. He looks a bit rough around the edges."

Alex laughed. "That's an understatement."

"Does he live nearby?" Francie asked.

"A few blocks that way." Alex pointed toward the shoreline. He glanced first at Francie, then at Holiday. "Are we still on a date?"

"Nah, that wrapped up a few minutes ago," Holiday informed him.

"It's not you, it's me." Francie winked. "Truly and honestly."

"You did your part and then some," Holiday added. "Nobody's blaming you."

"And there's no need to pretend you're disappointed." Francie raised one perfectly sculpted brow. "I know you didn't feel any chemistry, either."

Alex looked as though he was torn between being elated and insulted. "So all you want from me is my brother's number?"

"An introduction would be very much appreciated." Francie stood up and strolled back into the barroom to get her coat. "I've booked my room through New Year's Day. What can I say? I was feeling optimistic."

"I'll text everyone in the next day or two and we can get a proper date on the calendar," Holiday volunteered.

"You're off duty, remember?" Francie said. "Alex and I can manage this all by ourselves. Your assistance is no longer required."

Holiday recognized the truth of this on an intellectual level, but she also knew that as soon as she stopped being the concierge, she would have to start texting her family members to let them know she wouldn't be home by morning. She'd have to look at Alex and see the man who wanted to make her wishes come true instead of the man she'd sidelined for someone else. She'd have to stop dealing with everyone else's problems and start dealing with her own. *No, thank you.*

"Do you need a place to stay tonight?" Alex asked Holiday. "If you need a spare bedroom—"

"Oh, I'll be fine." She started cleaning up the kitchen.

"I'm going to need the specifics," he pressed. "You checked out of the inn this morning, right? So, where are you going to be tonight?"

"I'll figure something out." She walked away from him and back into the barroom.

He stayed right on her heels. "You're welcome to stay at my place."

She steadied herself with one hand on the doorframe. Did he mean . . .

"I can bunk at Paul's or my mom's," he added. "I'm going to be on Zoom half the night. I can do that anywhere."

He did not.

"Thank you," she muttered. "That's very kind. But I'll figure something out."

"You can stay with me," Francie offered. "The innkeeper mentioned I've got an extra sofa in my guest room. You're more than welcome." She gave a quick nod to denote that the matter was settled. "I am not going to leave my Wish Granter stranded on Christmas Eve. This is part of my new, free-spirited lifestyle. Reservations not required."

Holiday felt her resolve disintegrating. "I am really tired." And discouraged. And in need of some time and space to figure out what to do about Alex. At this point, her confusion and fatigue were fueling a downward spiral.

"Come along, then." Francie rewrapped her scarf with precision. "We'll get some extra blankets and pillows."

Holiday fell into step behind her, only to be intercepted by Alex, who placed both of his hands on Holiday's forearms. He looked at her. She looked at him.

"Sorry about the sweater," she murmured. "Paul told me about the Christmas Eve wardrobe breakup."

At this, Alex's whole body tensed. "I'm going to kill him."

"He was trying to help."

"*Kill* him." Alex's eyes went huge as another thought occurred. "What else did he tell you?"

Holiday turned away to blow out the cranberry-scented candles. "Um . . . not much."

"Listen." He lowered his voice so Francie couldn't hear. "We need to talk. But I really do need to get on some calls tonight. I'm sorry, but I—"

"No need to apologize." This time, she reached out for him. "If anyone understands the need to work on Christmas Eve, it's me."

"I *am* sorry that you're missing Christmas morning with your family because of me," he said.

She shrugged. "I'm missing it because of me. I knew the risks of this deal going in."

"Holiday." He reached up and brushed a stray curl back from her forehead. "Can't you let this one thing be personal?"

She leaned into his touch for a moment. "Fine. I blame you, one hundred percent."

"Thank you." Alex stepped away and raised his voice. "You're invited to my place for breakfast in the morning. Both of you."

"I can't." Holiday shook her head amid an odd blend of anticipation and disappointment. "I'm going to have to get on the road as soon as it stops snowing." She checked the projected overnight weather. "Which should be around four a.m."

"Stop talking nonsense." Francie put her hands on her hips. "No one is leaving this island at four a.m."

"The earliest the bridge will be open is seven," Alex said. Perhaps sensing that Holiday was a lost cause, he appealed to Francie. "Paul will be at breakfast tomorrow."

"Then so will we," Francie replied. "What time would you like us to come by? And what can we bring?"

"Eight o'clock. And nothing."

Holiday shot Alex a warning look. "And you better not kill Paul before Francie has a chance to meet him."

"I'll hold off until eight-fifteen," he agreed. "After that, I make no promises."

"Fair enough." With every strand of twinkle lights Holiday unplugged, her eyes felt heavier. She wanted to drag herself back to the pink palace, sleep for fourteen hours, and wake up with her world back to normal. Except Alex. She still wanted Alex there. But she'd be better equipped to figure out all her feelings and what to do about them after she slept for fourteen hours. "Excuse me for a moment; I have to make a phone call." She ducked back into the kitchen and dialed her sister's number. No answer. Then she dialed her parents. Straight to voice mail. So she had to settle for sending them all a text:

Stuck in Maine due to storm of the century. I'll get on the road as soon as I can tomorrow. I love you guys and I am so so so so SO sorry to miss Christmas morning with you. Nora, get my jammies ready, and we'll wear them tomorrow night.

She hit "send" and stared at the darkening screen, hoping that someone would respond immediately, telling her it was fine and all was forgiven. But there was no reply. They were probably gathered in the living room together, playing a game or watching a movie, not staring obsessively at their phones.

When she reentered the bar, Alex was on his phone. He turned away and lowered his voice when he saw her. She locked the bar's front door and shooed him out the back.

"Go home," she told him. "Do your business deal thing. We're all good here."

He covered his mouthpiece. "Do you need a ride to the inn?"

"No, it's like three doors down." She physically pushed him out the door. "Thanks for everything. Bye."

The last thing she glimpsed in his expression as he retreated to the parking lot was . . . *relief?*

"All right, spill it." Francie pounced as soon as Holiday returned to the barroom. "What's going on between you and Alex?"

Holiday's mystified expression was genuine this time. "I wish I knew."

"Oh, come on. You can tell me. We're going to be roomies!"

"He's working on some sort of business deal," Holiday said. "At this hour on Christmas Eve. That's all I know."

"But the way you two were looking at each other." Francie paused. "Or rather, *not* looking at each other. It's like you're the girl he had a crush on in high school and never worked up the nerve to approach. And I would know."

Holiday couldn't shake that final image of his face. How happy he'd been to leave. How quickly he'd strode to his truck without a backward glance. But that was on her. He'd done everything she'd asked of him, plus more. So when she'd told him to back off and he did . . . well, wasn't that exactly what she'd said she'd wanted?

"I just need to get off this island and back to real life." Holiday wiped down the bar one more time. "And you really don't have to put me up on your sofa. I have a friend I can call—"

"Don't you worry. There's plenty of room at the inn." Francie prepared to open the back door and step into the snowbanks. "Ready to participate in the amateur Ice Capades?"

Holiday checked her phone one more time. Still no messages from her family. "Ready as I'll ever be."

Chapter Twenty

WHEN HOLIDAY OPENED her eyes the next morning, there was sufficient sunlight to see the cascade of pink ruffles surrounding her. She turned over on the sofa, which, despite all the tufting and tassels, had proved a cozy little bunk for the night.

The bed was rumpled, but empty. Francie was nowhere to be seen. Holiday checked the time: 7:12 a.m. As she sat up, the door opened, and Francie strolled in with two pottery mugs stacked precariously in one hand.

"Special delivery." She handed a cup of coffee to Holiday. "Santa brought you caffeine."

"God bless us, every one." Holiday sipped the warm brew and felt her synapses spark to life. The sun filtering in through the lace curtains boded well for the weather. "I wonder if they've opened the bridge yet."

A cursory check of her phone revealed no updates, either about the status of the bridge or her family. Frowning, Holiday dialed her sister and mother in succession—still to no avail.

"Okay, I've got to go." Holiday threw the covers aside and stood. "My whole family has ghosted me, which really isn't their style. I need to get on the road and figure out what the heck is happening."

"Not so fast," Francie said. "We promised we'd stop by Alex's place, remember?"

"Eh, I remember." Holiday rubbed the back of her neck, which had apparently gotten wedged amid the throw pillows at an awkward angle. "But I don't want to."

"Because there's nothing going on between you two?"

"There's either nothing going on or too much going on, and I don't know how to deal with either scenario." Holiday's phone chimed, sparing her from any further interrogation. "Thank goodness—it's my sister." She pressed the phone to her ear. "Proof of life?"

"I could ask the same of you," Nora shot back. "The bridge closed? A likely story."

"It's true! I have witnesses!"

"Yes, well, tell all your witnesses to prepare to be deposed when we put you on trial for blowing us off after all those empty promises. Mom is a formidable prosecutor."

"I will be home by dinner," Holiday vowed.

"Stop right there," Nora commanded. "Can we not do this again? Instead of making unkeepable promises about where you'll be and when, just take a breath, get yourself together, and come home at a reasonable pace when it's safe to do so. How about that?"

"How mad is Mom?" Holiday asked.

"You know Mom. She's not mad, just—"

Holiday cringed. "Disappointed?"

"Bingo."

"Kill me now."

"No need," Nora trilled. "Mom will take care of that when you finally get over here."

"Well, I can't say I didn't earn it." Holiday took another sip of coffee. "And, Nora? Next time I swear up and down and left and right that I'm going to make it home for Christmas—"

"Tell you to shut your lying mouth?"

"Yeah. That'd be great."

Nora laughed. "Will do. We'll see you when we see you. And drive carefully."

"Well, that was humiliating." Holiday finished her coffee in a few quick gulps. "My New Year's resolution is going to be to look at my life, look at my choices."

"I did that last New Year's," Francie said. "That's why I'm here. Snowed in on an island, about to spin-off a blind date. Here's an idea—look at your life and your choices while you get dressed. Time's a-wasting." She paused, her coffee mug halfway to her mouth, as she noticed a small, gilt-framed cross-stitched peony tucked away in the corner. "Isn't that beautiful? The stitches are so tiny, it almost looks like watercolor."

Holiday hadn't even noticed the piece due to the profusion of toile and pastels covering every inch of the walls. "It is beautiful." She stepped closer to examine the piece. "It'd be a great gift for someone who likes cross-stitch pieces." She tapped her fingernail on the gilt frame as inspiration struck. "Hey, when you went down to the lobby for coffee, was Michelina at the front desk?"

"I don't know her name, but there was a lady with white

hair and lots of jewelry."

"That's Michelina." Holiday threw on a fluffy white robe, eased the cross-stich off the wall, and grabbed her wallet. "I'm going to go make her an offer she can't refuse."

"But what about breakfast?" Francie cried.

"I'll be right back." Holiday grabbed her cell phone, too, as she headed for the door. "Because it turns out, the Wish Granter is never truly off duty."

She dialed the phone on her way down to the lobby. "Merry Christmas to my favorite small-town genealogist. Let me ask you a question, just out of curiosity . . . Did you ever find a great gift for your mom? No? Well, it's your lucky day. I'm heading out of town as soon as possible, but I've got something for you before I go . . . I don't want to spoil the surprise. Meet me at Alex's house at eight o'clock."

"ARE WE GETTING close?" Holiday asked as she and Francie slogged down the middle of the snowy road. "GPS says we're getting close."

"Okay, the address is 17 Spruce Street." Francie peered at the houses, which were increasingly widely spaced as they approached the shoreline. "It would be helpful if everything wasn't covered in snow."

"Maybe it's that driveway down there?" Holiday pointed out a mailbox in the distance.

"I can't believe you haven't been to Alex's house yet." Francie shot a sidelong glance at Holiday. "It sounds like you've been everywhere else with him."

"Just New Hampshire."

Francie smiled slyly. "In the olden days, that would mean you're now engaged."

"Thank you, Edith Wharton." Holiday started brushing snow off the mailboxes to discover the addresses and realized that Alex must reside at the end of this long and winding driveway that disappeared behind a thick copse of pine trees. She took a tentative step off the main road. Her leg sank into the snow, which completely enveloped her knee-high leather boots. "Next time I come to Maine, I'm definitely bringing a snowsuit. With mitten clips and everything."

Francie tromped into the snow right behind her. Luckily, there were two fresh tire tracks, which provided an easy trail to follow all the way to the front porch of the expansive house constructed of timber and rough-hewn logs. A small curlicue of smoke rose from the stone chimney, lacing the breeze with the slight smell of burning wood.

"So, the man basically lives in a ski lodge," Francie observed. And indeed, Alex's home, while rustic and welcoming, was undeniably large. Double walls of windows offered glimpses of the icy ocean on the opposite side of the house.

"The heating bills must be astronomical," Holiday said. "But it's lovely."

"Hey!" Janine rounded the corner, jogging in an attempt to catch up. She'd traded in her customary flannel pants and high-tops for black pants, black boots, and a black mohair coat. She stopped in her tracks when she saw Francie. "Hi.

Who are you?"

"Francine Penewate." Francie offered a handshake and a dimpled smile. "Pleased to meet you."

"She's the blind date from last night," Holiday explained.

Janine took a moment to absorb this. "And now you two are both having breakfast at Alex's house?"

"It didn't work out," Holiday said.

"Don't be so hasty." Francie fluffed her hair and announced, "Alex isn't the right match for me, but I have high hopes for his brother."

Janine turned to Holiday. "So what's the big reveal? This better be good. I got up early on a holiday and dressed like a real person."

"You sure did." Holiday grinned. "What are you, the Noël Ninja?"

Janine flushed and adjusted her coat lapels. "I've never been to a multimillionaire's house, but I figured you can't go wrong with basic black."

"You're absolutely right," Francie assured her.

"I look good," Janine informed Holiday. "And ninja chic is what I'm going for. Always."

Holiday reached into her purse and pulled out the framed cross-stitch, which she'd hastily wrapped in a few old pages of Michelina's ledger.

"What's this?" Janine regarded the package with open suspicion.

"A very thoughtful present from you to your mother."

Janine untaped a corner of the wrapping with the precision of a seasoned gift-peeker. "Holy kittens, she's going to love this."

"I thought she might." Holiday basked in the glow of a gift well given.

"No, seriously, she's going to *love* it. And she never likes anything I give her." Janine almost looked as though she might shed a tear.

"Until now." Holiday's excitement got the better of her. "And you know that cute little craft store next to the bakery? I saw a sign in the window—they're offering some embroidery classes this spring. Maybe you could sign her up for a Mother's Day gift."

"Genius."

"Maybe you could take the class with her!" Francie exclaimed.

Janine balked at this. "No offense, but you've never met my mother."

"Well, if she raised a daughter like you, she must be . . ." Francie trailed off as she saw Janine's expression. "I'll just worry about Paul and leave your mother to you."

Janine gave her a thumbs-up, then turned back to Holiday. "What do I owe you?"

Holiday recoiled at the very suggestion. "Nothing! You helped me hunt down Driscoll Davidson's long-lost grandnephew"—she tried to remember the exact familial link—"or something. You drove me all over Maine and helped me find the best spot in town for the blind date. You dressed up like a real person to meet me here! I couldn't have done any of this without you. A measly cross-stitched peony is the least that I can do."

Janine started to protest, so Holiday conceded, "But if you insist, you can come to breakfast with us. It's going to be awkward, but it'll be slightly less awkward with you there."

"All hail the Noël Ninja." Janine tucked the package into her coat pocket.

Chapter Twenty-One

THE THREE OF them made it up the front steps, which had been freshly salted and sanded, and stomped across the porch floor in a vain attempt to shake the snow from their boots. Holiday could feel the snow melting into her jeans. Rivulets of ice snaked down the insides of her boots. As she raised her finger to ring the doorbell, Francie stopped her with a hand on Holiday's sleeve.

"Shhh. Do you hear that?" Francie whispered.

They stilled and listened to the strains of music coming from within. Every few seconds, the music was punctuated by what sounded like raucous laughter.

"Is he having a party in there?" Janine murmured.

"At this hour of the morning? Maybe he just invited a bunch of people over after the wine bar last night and kept going with the mulled wine," Francie theorized.

"His entire staff from Boston could be chilling by the fireplace," Janine said.

"No, they can't," Francie countered. "The bridge was closed all night."

"We're about to find out." Holiday took charge and rang the bell. "And let's look on the bright side—I bet he's got the pantry stocked with really excellent snacks."

After waiting for at least thirty seconds for Alex to answer the door, Holiday rang again. "I'm counting to ten, and then I'm out of here," she told her companions. "Ten . . . nine . . . eight . . ."

The massive front door swung inward, revealing a petite woman with silver-streaked blond hair and sweater completely covered in copper sequins. "Good morning. Come in, come in." She stepped back and beckoned Holiday, Janine, and Francie into a foyer featuring a soaring ceiling crisscrossed with lumber beams and a massive wrought-iron light fixture. "You must be Holiday, and you're Francie, right?"

"Right on both counts," Francie confirmed.

"This is Janine." Holiday dragged Janine to the fore.

"I'm the librarian," Janine said.

"Welcome. I'm Grace, Alex and Paul's mom." The woman gestured to a pile of wet boots resting on a two-tiered wooden rack as she closed the door. "Kick off your shoes and come on in."

The party atmosphere was in full effect—Ella Fitzgerald's "Winter Wonderland" on the stereo, underscored by the sound of glasses clinking, excited chatter coming from the next room, and the singular, delicious, unmistakable smell of . . .

Holiday gasped.

The other women turned to her. Grace looked elated, Francie and Janine looked confused.

It couldn't be. It wasn't possible.

"What?" Janine hissed.

Before her better judgment could overrule her mouth,

Holiday called out, "*Mom*?"

"Well, well, well. Look what the blizzard blew in." Cecelia Smith strolled into the foyer, decked out in flannel pajamas and holding a mimosa in one hand.

"Mom!" Holiday flung herself at her mother, heedless of her snow-flecked coat and sopping wet hair. "I knew I smelled your cinnamon rolls!"

"Hi, honey." Her mother gave her a squeeze and a kiss on the cheek. "You girls are like bloodhounds with those cinnamon rolls." She rolled her eyes at Grace. "I spoiled them growing up, I'm afraid."

Grace laughed. "I can relate."

Holiday literally hopped with excitement. "Who else is here? Is Dad here? Is Nora here?"

"There are cinnamon rolls and bottomless mimosas," Holiday's sister drawled as she stepped into the foyer. "So, of course I'm here. I'm here and I'm never leaving." Nora, who had selected a jolly peppermint-stripe pattern for her pajamas, joined in on the hug.

Francie stood back, bewildered. "Is my mom here too?"

"Is *my* mom here?" Janine froze, one boot on and one boot off, ready to flee.

"I'm afraid not, but don't worry. We're all family today," Grace assured her. "Come into the living room and we'll explain everything."

But Holiday couldn't wait a nanosecond more. "Is this real life?" She pinched her own cheek before poking her mom and sister again to ascertain their physical reality. "How did you get here? When? Who? The bridge . . ."

"Only people wearing flannel pajamas get the juicy details." Nora pointed to a powder room across the foyer. "Better hurry up." She introduced herself to Francie and Janine with "I'm the cool sister. We have a few spare Christmas jammies if you'd like some. Would you prefer snowflakes or Christmas light design?"

"Um, snowflakes, I guess." Francie had clearly made a decision to just go with whatever was unfolding.

"Do you have anything with yetis or Heat Miser, things of that nature?" Janine asked.

"Sadly, we do not," Nora said.

"Then I'll stick with my current ensemble." Janine proceeded to take off her second boot.

"Suit yourself. So, Holiday, you get the Christmas light pattern. The faster you put them on, the faster you get a cinnamon roll."

"Come on, Francie, you can have a few bites while she's getting changed." Cecelia put her arm around Francie's shoulders and led her away. "You look famished."

"Now that you mention it, I am hungry." Francie motioned for Janine to join them.

Holiday was still standing and staring in the middle of the entryway. "Alex? Are you in here somewhere?"

"Stop it," her sister admonished. "He's not coming in here. He's under strict instructions to stay in the living room until."

"Until what?" Holiday prompted.

"Until you're ready to handle the truth." Nora gave her a little push in the direction of the powder room. "Now put some hustle in your bustle and get changed."

Holiday stripped off her sodden jeans and shimmied into a pair of shapeless, oversized pajamas as quickly as possible. Her sister had even laid out a pair of fuzzy, white faux-fur slippers to complete the ensemble.

"Okay, I'm ready." Holiday raced out of the powder room, holding an armful of clothes. "Spill your guts."

"Your guest still has to put on her pajamas." Nora, who was clearly relishing every moment of sisterly torture, shook her head. "Where are your manners?"

Holiday practically gnashed her teeth as Francie stepped back into the foyer with a little dab of icing on the corner of her mouth. "How fast can you change?"

"It'll be like the Formula One pit stop of clothes." Francie darted into the powder room. "Time me!"

Holiday peered over her sister's shoulder, desperate for a glimpse of the rest of the party. "Alex? Dad?"

"Ignore her!" Nora yelled.

"I'm here, sweetie," replied the unmistakable voice of her father.

"Dad!" Nora cried. "You're ruining the surprise."

"Hi, Dad!" Holiday lowered her voice and assured Nora, "Don't worry, I'm surprised."

"Done!" Francie burst out of the powder room, her hair swept into a neat bun and her makeup still perfectly applied. "Pass the mimosas."

"Follow me." Grace linked arms with Francie and led her into the living room.

Holiday's jaw dropped. "How come she gets to waltz

right in and I'm stuck in here like the TSA line at the airport?"

"She's not my sister, so I'm not the boss of her," Nora said. "*You*, on the other hand . . . here, put on this blindfold."

Holiday evaded her sister's grasp and darted around her. The time for blindfolds and suspense had passed. She raced into an airy, rustic great room featuring a roaring fire in the massive fireplace and a ceiling-scraping, minimalist-decorated Christmas tree towering over the proceedings.

"Told ya." Francie had already snuggled into a plush chair-and-a-half by the hearth. "It is, in fact, a ski lodge."

Janine sat down beside her and kicked her feet up onto a leather ottoman. "I could get used to this."

Alex got up from the nearest sofa and offered Holiday a mimosa in a fancy crystal flute. "Merry Christmas."

Holiday ignored the drink for a moment and hugged her father, who was standing next to the fireplace. "Dad! I'm so glad you guys are here!"

"Well, we finally accepted the fact that if we'd like to spend Christmas morning together, we're going to have to come to you." Her dad kissed her temple, and Holiday soaked in the comforting scent of the shaving cream he'd been using since she was a child.

"Ugh, way to ruin the dramatic entrance." Nora trailed in, joined by Cecelia, who said, "Don't bicker, girls. It's Christmas."

Holiday planted her fuzzy-slippered feet on the woven red-and-white rug and demanded, "How? How did this happen?"

Nora pointed over at Alex. "Ask the man in the high-end pajamas."

Alex, who was wearing black-and-green-plaid pants with a red-and-navy-plaid shirt, defended himself. "Not all of us have matching flannel pajamas, okay? I did the best I could, considering I had zero notice."

"Don't tell him what to wear," advised Paul, who was hanging out on the window seat across the room. "It always ends badly."

Alex offered the mimosa to Holiday again. "Here. You're going to need this for the story we're about to tell you."

Holiday took his word for it and treated herself to a little sip as she sank into a huge down pillow next to the coffee table. "Ooh, is this fresh orange juice?"

"Squeezed it myself," Paul boasted.

"Good morning," Holiday said to him. "Merry Christmas. I assume you've met Francie?"

"I have not." But he'd been staring at her since the moment Holiday walked in the room.

"Why don't you introduce yourself while I figure out what the heck is going on." Holiday lifted her chin at Francie. "That's Paul. The pilot brother."

Paul stood up. "That's right. I'm the pilot brother. You've heard about me?"

"A bit." Francie batted her eyelashes. "But I'd love to hear more."

"Here." Janine got to her feet and motioned to Paul. "Switch seats with me."

Holiday beheld Alex in all his plaid-clashing glory. "This is the real reason why you left corporate America, isn't it? You figured out how to teleport."

"I wish I could take credit for that, but no. The truth is much less exciting."

"False," Nora interjected. "Flying in your private jet is *very* exciting."

Holiday put down her glass.

Alex laughed at her expression. "It's not my jet. It's my company's jet. They just let me borrow it for the night."

"But when . . ."

"In the middle of the night!" Nora clapped her hand to her chest. "He called us as soon as you found out the bridge was closed."

"So that's who you were all talking to when I was trying to call last night?" Holiday asked Nora. "You—and Mom and Dad—blew me off on Christmas Eve to scheme with a stranger? How could you?"

"The stranger has a private jet." Nora shrugged. "I'm easily bought."

"We didn't want to ruin the surprise," Cecelia soothed.

Holiday turned back to Alex. "This is . . . a lot to take in."

He sat down next to her. "I know."

"I mean, last time I saw you, you looked . . ." She searched for the right word.

"Stressed?" he suggested. "Overwhelmed with logistics?"

"Yeah, but also . . ."

"Super-great in the sweater you picked out?" he volun-

BETH KENDRICK

teered.

She clapped her hand to her forehead. "I am never picking out a sweater for you again."

"Yes, you are," he informed her. "Every year. It'll be our Christmas tradition."

Somewhere in the background, a woman—Francie?—sighed swoonily at the idea of this.

"You looked relieved," she whispered. "You practically ran away from me."

He took a sip of her mimosa and handed the glass back to her. "I had to work quickly if I was going to pull this off."

"We almost didn't make it," her mother informed her. "They were debating closing all the airports, but we managed to land in Portland."

"But how'd you get out to Alemos?" Holiday still couldn't puzzle that out. "Is there a private airport out here somewhere?"

"He's got a rusty old sea plane and a pilot who likes a challenge," Paul called from across the room.

Holiday gaped. "You all flew in a seaplane? With those winds?"

"Also very exciting!" Nora trilled.

"We made it here by . . . what? Five o'clock?" Her father checked his watch. "It was an adventure."

"You all could have died!"

"Uh, hello, I'm right here." Paul looked miffed. "Not to brag, but I'm really good at what I do."

"I bet you are," Francie purred.

"We didn't die," Cecelia pointed out. "We're all here safe

214

and sound, thanks to Alex and Paul."

Alex locked his gaze with Holiday's. "And you kept your promise—you're spending Christmas morning with your family."

Grace laughed. "You boys are exactly like your father. Full of surprises." She told Cecelia, "Just the other day, they lay in wait and sneaked in to decorate my whole house while I ran errands."

Alex sucked in his breath while he, Paul, Holiday, and Janine exchanged a flurry of meaningful glances.

"What?" Grace demanded. "What's going on?"

"Nothing," Paul said, much too loudly.

"Don't give me that." Grace set her champagne flute down on the mantel with a clink. "Those are guilty looks if ever I saw them." She rounded on Paul. "What did you do this time?"

Paul threw up his hands. "Why do you assume I'm the one who did something?"

"It's always you," Alex said drily.

Paul appealed to Francie. "This is what happens when you're the good-looking maverick of the family."

"I can relate." Francie sipped her drink and sat back to enjoy the show.

"Well?" Grace looked surprisingly formidable for a tiny blonde clad in sequins. "Confess."

"Nothing to confess, just another Christmas surprise." Alex pulled out a silver gift bag from under the tree. "I was going to give this to you later, but since you brought it up . . . Merry Christmas, Mom."

Everyone crowded around Grace as she pulled out layer after layer of white tissue paper.

Janine nudged Holiday. Holiday nudged Janine.

Francie asked Paul to explain what was going on, which he took as an opportunity to snuggle up close and whisper in her ear.

Grace gasped as she pulled out the red-glass masterpiece. After cradling it in both palms for a moment, she lifted it high to catch the morning sunlight.

"That is gorgeous," Cecelia breathed.

"Stunning," Francie echoed.

"Nice job," Janine mouthed over Grace's shoulder. Nora noticed this and waggled her eyebrows at Holiday, who made a big show of looking clueless.

"Is this . . ." Grace lowered the star to inspect it more closely. Then she regarded her sons with a mixture of love and awe. "Where did you find this?"

"I finally went through the rest of the boxes in my garage," Alex said.

"I helped." Paul was still speaking a touch too loudly.

"And wouldn't you know it? There it was, underneath some tinsel."

"Just in time for Christmas." Paul leaned over to hug his mother. "Aren't you—"

"Hang on." Grace's gaze sharpened, and she fended him off. "Don't touch."

The ping-pong of meaningful gazes recommenced.

"This is real." Grace traced the outline of a glass pane with one finger. "This is a Driscoll Davidson."

"Ooh, let me see." Nora wriggled her way into the fray to examine the piece. "It sure is, and it's a beauty."

"Nora would know." Her father's voice was tinged with pride. "She was an art history major."

Grace handed the glass star to Nora. "This is a real Driscoll Davidson? You're sure?"

"I mean, I'd have to hire an authenticator to be one hundred percent positive, but it looks real to me." Nora whipped around to Holiday. "It looks real to you?"

"Yep." Holiday stepped sideways to hide behind Alex.

"Of course it's real." He kept a perfect poker face. "I told you, I found it in your boxes."

Grace shook her head. "I don't know where you boys found this, but it was not in my boxes."

The color drained from Paul's face. Francie clutched his hand in support.

"The star in my box, the star that your father and I put on top of the tree every year, was a replica," Grace informed them. She let that sink in for a moment before continuing. "This star in my hands is a real Driscoll Davidson. We could never have afforded that."

"But . . ." Alex sputtered. "But you said your rich uncle Morton . . ."

"My uncle Morton was a cheapskate to the core. That's why he was so rich!" Grace scoffed. "He gave us a fake Davidson, and we all knew it."

"*We* didn't know it," Alex pointed out.

"We sure didn't," Paul said.

"Well, what difference did it make?" Grace looked exasperated. "Real or replica, it was special to us because it was our first Christmas in our first house."

"Oh." Alex picked at the sleeve of his plaid shirt.

"Now we know," Paul concluded. "Mom, if you'll just let me see that for a quick second—" He reached for the glass star.

Grace snatched it away. "Don't you dare. I don't know what you kids did with the replica, but you're not getting anywhere near the real one!" She turned to Nora. "You may look at it, if you'd like."

"I'd love to." Nora oohed and aahed over the craftsmanship.

Grace pointed her finger at Alex, then Paul. "Honestly. What were you thinking?" Before they could mumble apologies, she added, "That star must have cost a fortune!"

"Just my dignity," Alex admitted.

Holiday had to grin at the memory of Alex in his Santa hat and elf shoes.

"Well, it was worth it." Grace finally smiled. "But you're never going to lay a finger on it again."

"No, ma'am," they chorused.

Janine watched all this in slack-jawed amazement. "Is this how normal families do Christmas every year?"

Cecelia laughed. "Did you hear that? She called us normal."

"I mean, all this time, I thought my family was the only one that spent Christmas knee-deep in chaos and confusion," Janine added.

"Of course not." Grace regarded Janine with dismay.

"You could still call your mom and invite her over for breakfast." Holiday turned to Alex. "Right?"

He nodded. "The more the merrier."

Janine nibbled her lower lip. "Well . . ."

"Do it," Francie urged. "I'll sit next to you and be your conversational buffer."

"And I'll sit next to Francie," Paul volunteered.

"Perfect. It's settled." Francie refilled Janine's mimosa. "Make the call."

"What the heck? It's Christmas." Janine pulled out her phone, setting off a round of applause.

While Holiday's parents admired the glass star with Nora and Grace, and Paul and Francie provided Janine with moral support, Alex took Holiday's hand and pulled her back into the foyer.

He turned to look down at her as the sunlight streamed through the skylight. It was so bright and clear that Holiday could see the exhaustion etched into the corners of his eyes, the toll that pulling off a miracle through a sleepless night had taken.

She reached up to cradle his cheek in the palm of her hand. "Thank you. Thank you for bringing my family to me. Thank you for everything."

"I have a lot to say to you." He wrapped his arms around her and pulled her close against his chest.

She nestled into the warm, strong contours of his body. "I have a lot to say to you too."

"But this is not the time for a long, serious discussion." He rested his chin on the top of her head. "Obviously."

She smiled into the crook of his neck as she listened to the chatter and laughter emanating from the next room.

"You've given me the best present I've ever gotten," she said. "Better than I could even imagine. This is . . . personal. Beyond personal."

He loosened his hold on her just a bit. "In a good way?"

She hugged him tighter. "In a way that makes it impossible not to fall in love." The words were out before she could think better of them, but she didn't care. He'd done so much for her. The least she could do was give him her trust and her truth.

He took a step back and captured both her hands in his. "I'm glad to hear that, because I have a proposal for you." His eyes gleamed with mischief as he watched her face.

She had to remind herself to breathe.

"You love your job, right? And you're great at your job." He squeezed her hands. "But December twenty-fifth is somewhat of an arbitrary day for a celebration, is it not?"

Holiday tilted her head as she tried to decipher his meaning. "I'd say it's a pretty hard deadline."

"For your clients," he allowed. "You said it yourself—every year, we drive ourselves nuts trying to do everything and see everyone based on that one date on the calendar." He pulled her close again. "I say we shake things up a bit. I say we take all of this—the family, the food, the chaos—and we move it to March."

She started to laugh. "March?"

"Or May. Whenever. Your choice. We'll pick a week in spring to get everyone together."

"Christmas in July." She grinned as she started to imagine what this could entail.

"Christmas whenever you say. All of the joy, none of the stress."

"We could go to the beach. Or rent a big house in a big city every year." She let herself dream big. "Cranberries freeze well. We could buy them in December and put them on ice until June. We could buy Christmas jammies on sale on December twenty-sixth and save them 'til August."

"No problem," he assured her. "We'll just crank up the AC."

She couldn't stop smiling. "You know what? Everyone was right about you. You are a great guy. And a genius."

"Maybe," he allowed. "But more importantly, I'm your Christmas concierge."

"You are." Her smile wilted a bit as anxiety set in. "But you . . . you don't think you'll change your mind about all this before March or May or July?"

"No." There was no hesitation.

"I mean, I don't even know where I'll be going one week to the next. I live in hotels and airports for six months out of the year."

He shrugged. "Okay. I can go with you, or I can stay here. I live for logistics."

"And it's not always luxury in Paris and New York." She nibbled her lower lip. "Sometimes, it's nonglamorous towns in the middle of nowhere."

"Like Alemos Island, Maine?" he teased.

"I'm just saying I'm not exactly traditional. Whatever we

have together . . ."

"You're falling in love," he reminded her. "Too late to take it back."

"It won't look like everybody else's love story. It probably won't feel like everybody else's love story, either."

"Then my wish is granted. And I have one more thing to say." He paused. "Actually, I have something I'd like *you* to say."

For a moment, they stood silently, their hearts beating against one another through a few thin layers of flannel.

"Anything," Holiday whispered.

He placed his lips against her temple and murmured, "I want you to admit that I've out-wish-granted the Wish Granter."

She burst out laughing, but he held her close.

"Admit defeat. You can't deny it."

And he was right. She closed her eyes and smelled the cinnamon, felt the warmth of the fire radiating across the room, listened to the laughter of the people they loved. And she had to confess, "You're right." She slipped her arms around his neck and added, "You may have won this round, but just wait 'til next year."

"You're on." He moved his lips from her ear to her mouth to seal that promise with a kiss.

THE END

Join Tule Publishing's newsletter for more great reads and weekly deals!

If you enjoyed *The Christmas Concierge*, you'll love these other Tule Christmas books!

The Christmas Blueprint
by Sinclair Jayne

The X-Mas Club
by Lenora Worth

Once Upon a Christmas
by Jane Porter

The Christmas Clues
by Scarlet Wilson

Available now at your favorite online retailer!

About the Author

Beth Kendrick is the author of 17 novels, including
Nearlyweds, which was adapted for a Hallmark Channel
original movie. As the owner of a Portuguese Water Dog and
a Spinone Italiano, she is on her way to becoming an official
Crazy Dog Lady. Beth recently relocated with her family to
the Tahoe area, where she is looking forward to the
possibility of white Christmases.

Thank you for reading

The Christmas Concierge

If you enjoyed this book, you can find more from all our great authors at TulePublishing.com, or from your favorite online retailer.